I'm cyfaill y Prifardd Tom Parry-Jones
i ddiolch iddo am lawer "seiad" felys,
ac i Olwen, i ddiolch iddi hithau
am ei chroeso cyson ini fel teulu,

J. Ellis Williams,
Awst 15, 1973.

MURDER AT THE EISTEDDFOD

Murder at the Eisteddfod

A detective story in a new setting

J. Ellis Williams

GOMER PRESS
1973

First Impression - - *August 1973*

SBN 85088 216 8

Printed by
J. D. Lewis & Sons Ltd., Gomerian Press, Llandysul

Contents

PART ONE

THE MURDER

1. Prologue in a Pub

Detective Inspector Richard Hopkyn, sitting on the small oak settle in the corner beyond the fireplace, raised his tankard, blew a hole in the creamy top which capped his pint, and drank deep.

Yes, he said to himself, it's good honest beer, drawn straight from the wood. Perhaps, though, I shouldn't have ordered this third pint in the early morning. And yet, dammit, why not ? I'm on holiday. To hell with Scotland Yard ! Today, this week, next week, I'm a private citizen, with the right to enjoy myself. It's good beer, it's a good pub, and I'm enjoying myself more than I've done for years. I'm glad I came to the Eisteddfod, and I'll never miss another National Eisteddfod as long as I live.

A raised voice from the bar drew his attention. It came from a wiry-looking little man wearing a black bow-tie with pink spots.

"I'm telling you, man," he asserted to his companion, "there's only one male voice choir in Wales today which is first class. An' that's the Morriston Male Voice ! I've sung in that choir for ten years, an' I know what I'm talking about."

His companion in the woollen shirt and knitted scarf was not intimidated. He stretched out a gnarled and lean forefinger, and prodded the other in his double-fronted vest.

"Let me tell you this, my friend," he replied. "I was singing with the Ystalyfera Male Voice when you was crying for a clean nappy, and when the old choirs sang at the Eisteddfod they lifted the roof off ! Your modern choirs couldn't lift the skin off a rice pudding."

The collier was on the point of explosion when Sam, the landlord, butted in.

"You're both right and you're both wrong," he said, his placid smile casting oil on the troubled waters. "I remember Ystalyfera at the height of their glory. No other choir could touch them . . ."

"You're right," said the woollen shirt.

"Dramatic, that's what they was," said Sam. "Full of fireworks their singing was. I'll never forget their *Martyrs of the Arena, The Crusaders, Crossing the Plain* . . ."

"Aye," said the woollen shirt, "it was grand singing."

"Those were pieces," continued Sam, "which called for a strong virile rendering, and the Ystalyfera Choir had the voices to put them over. I could feel the blood coursing through my veins as I listened to them. But then there came a change in the set pieces to be sung at the Eisteddfod. Quieter and more difficult they was . . ."

"More musical," said the black bow-tie with the pink spots.

"Rice pudding stuff," said the knitted scarf.

"Anyway, it was a different kind of music," said Sam, "and it called for a different kind of singing. Less robust, more controlled . . ."

"That's right," said the bow-tie.

"But if you asks me," said Sam, "which of the two was the better choir, I'll tell you straight—both of them was. It's just like this here beer. Some like the bitter, some like the mild. There's more kick in the bitter, and them who want a kick out of life prefer it to the mild. But them who come here for a spell of quiet and comfort from the troubled world outside, they drink mild. They're both good beer, but they appeal to different tastes. And it's the same with choirs. Do you agree with me, sir ?"

Sam had addressed his question to the third man who stood at the bar. He had been a most interested listener to the discussion, and had obviously enjoyed Sam's summing-up. Hopkyn looked at him, and unconsciously began to classify him. About sixty-five ; flowing white hair, worn rather long, regularly brushed ; close-cropped grey moustache ; wide brow and well-kept hands ; blue eyes that sparkled with amusement.

"A very wise summing-up, my friend," he said to Sam. "I have heard and enjoyed both choirs. They might perhaps cavil at your alcoholic analysis of their respective techniques, but . . ."

He stopped short, and listened. The other two customers also turned their heads to listen. So did Hopkyn.

From the room at the back of the inn, where a bigger bar catered for a larger public than the front room could accommodate, came the sound of singing.

Not an uncommon thing in a pub, mused Hopkyn. Beer often leads to singing, usually a maudlin moaning of the latest music-hall hits. But here, in this little pub in the heart of Wales, the people in the back room were singing a Welsh cantata. And they were singing it well.

Dyddiau dyn sydd fel glaswelltyn—the days of man are like the grasses of the field. The singing began in unison ; then the tenors broke away in a descant ; and then the deep notes of the basses repeated the opening phrases.

Eleven o'clock, mused Hopkyn, on a morning in August 1951, and a crowded bar in a small village pub singing a cantata. Where else on earth, except in Wales, could one hear such singing ?

"Good basses," commented the gentleman with the wavy white hair.

"Tenors a bit ragged," criticised the bow-tie.

The knitted scarf had been quiet for some time, studying the face of the white-haired customer. Now he turned to him, rather hesitatingly, like a man feeling the way with his foot before stepping out.

"Excuse me, sir," he asked, "but is your name Harris ?"

"It is," replied the wavy hair.

"Ted Harris, of Maesydref ?"

"That's right."

Both Sam and the bow-tie now turned towards him, the singing momentarily forgotten.

"Not *the* Ted Harris ?" asked Sam.

"Well," smiled Mr. Harris, "there are probably several Ted Harrises living in Maesydref."

"Yes, yes," said the bow-tie, rather impatiently, "but there's only one Ted Harris who won the tenor solo at the National three times running."

"Ah well," sighed Mr. Harris, but not at all sadly, "that's a good many years ago, my friend."

Sam banged his fist on the counter.

"As soon as you come in," he declared, "I knew there was something familiar about your face. Ted Harris! Man alive, I liked you better than Caruso! Mind you, I'm not saying for one moment that you had as good a voice as Caruso . . ."

"Not by a long way," smiled Mr. Harris.

"But I liked you better," continued Sam, "because I could understand the words, and knew what you was getting at. You an' Harry Lewis of Nelson was the best tenors in the world for me!"

"That's right," said the knitted scarf. "You an' Harry Lewis an' Jabez Balfour—never hear singing like that at the Eisteddfod nowadays."

"And me talking about singing, throwing my weight about too," said the bow-tie, "with Ted Harris listening an' taking it all in. Bloody fool, that's what I was."

"No, no," laughed Mr. Harris. "You made some very pertinent comments . . ."

Again he was cut short. The back-room door had opened suddenly, and with its opening came a surge of singing. With it entered a wild-eyed, red-haired young man in a sports-coat.

"Any tenors in here?" he demanded. "They're wanted in the back. The basses aren't too bad, but the tenors are a right scraggy lot. Good voices, mind, but they need pulling together."

He looked at Hopkyn.

"You a tenor, sir?"

Hopkyn shook his head, and turned to look at Mr. Harris. Knitted scarf and bow-tie also looked at him.

Mr. Harris stepped forward, half-bowed to the sports-coat, and spoke.

"I used to be a tenor," he said, "though I don't do much singing nowadays. But if you'll have me, I'll gladly join your choir in the back room."

"Good for you !" said the sports-coat. "What about you two ?"

"Do you know who he is ?" asked bow-tie. "He's Ted Harris, man !"

Sports-coat stopped short.

"Not *the* Ted Harris ?" he asked.

"That's right," said the knitted scarf.

"God Almighty !" said the sports-coat. "You just wait till I tell them ! Come on, sir ! Now we'll get some singing !"

He disappeared, and Mr. Harris followed him through the door. Bow-tie and knitted scarf paused a moment to look at each other. Then they silently finished their beer, and filed out after him.

This, said Hopkyn to himself, is Wales : this is the Eisteddfod. If I were one of those reporters covering the Eisteddfod for a foreign newspaper, and wished to describe the spirit of the Eisteddfod to people who had never seen or felt it, I wouldn't begin with the huge pavilion in the Eisteddfod grounds, nor with the ten thousand audience packed inside it, nor with the hurry and the bustle and the traffic and the hurly-burly. No. I'd start with this little backwater of a pub, and describe how the Eisteddfod tide floods into all the alleys and byways of this little town, filling and overflowing it, so that wherever one goes, be it pavilion or chapel vestry or restaurant or school or one of the scores of little tents and caravans dotted over the countryside for miles around, the Eisteddfod laps its way into every nook and cranny, filling the air with music.

I'm repeating myself, he said. It's time I went out for a walk.

2. Invasion

The street outside was crowded, but it was a good-humoured, easy-going crowd. The Eisteddfod lasted all week, from nine o'clock in the morning until six in the evening ; and at seven o'clock there came a concert in the huge Eisteddfod pavilion, or if you preferred drama, a performance at the little Town Hall. There was no need for anyone to hurry : everybody could have his fill of culture before night fell.

Hopkyn paused underneath the arched entrance leading to the inn-yard, and looked at the throng ambling by. The bright staccato lilt of miners from the Rhondda, the soft drawling tones of farmers from Carmarthenshire, the broad guttural accents of quarrymen from Caernarvon-shire—they were all there, all the dialects from all over Wales, every vale and cwm and commote had its representatives in the endless concourse that passed along the narrow street.

For this week, Hopkyn said to himself, for just this one week, Rhyd-yr-Onnen is the Capital of Wales. It hasn't a Civic Centre like Cardiff, nor a University College like Aberystwyth, nor a Norman Castle like Caernarvon ; but for this one week, Rhyd-yr-Onnen is the undisputed Capital of Wales.

What an experience it was for the little town, its population of four thousand all of a sudden multiplied by five ! Every house was full of visitors to the Eisteddfod. Chapel vestries and schools had been fitted with camp beds and turned into temporary hostels. The outlying villages had been combed for apartments. Tents and caravans sprawled over the countryside for miles around. Three immense marquees, each one capable of feeding over a thousand at a time, had been put up in the Eisteddfod grounds to cater for day visitors to the Eisteddfod. Cafes and restaurants, pubs and hotels, were full to overflowing. A week's mad hustle, a lunatic joyous mirthful exhilarating and maddeningly enjoyable week, and then Rhyd-yr-Onnen would again relapse into its normal quiet, would feel lonely and sad, as utterly exhausted as a drunkard on a Sunday morning after a week's hectic spree.

The Chief Constable had warned Hopkyn what to expect.

"Dear Hopkyn," he had written, "I hope you will not misunderstand me when I say that I was both glad and sorry to receive your letter. I was delighted to hear that you again propose to spend part of your annual leave in your native country, and that I shall have the pleasure of your company for at least a week of your holiday. I have looked forward with joyous expectancy to our annual re-union, and have spent the long winter nights experimenting with new flies for our trout fishing. I still insist, despite your arguments to the contrary, that the only colour which appeals to a trout is red ; and to prove my contention, I have this year prepared half a dozen specimens which combine various shades of scarlet, carmine, purple, and pink. A trout is an inquisitive creature, and I am confident that a fly which embodies all the shades of its favourite colour will excite its curiosity even if it does not feel very hungry at the time. Unfortunately, however, the fishing has been so poor up to now that I have not been able to test my theory in practice. A further predicament has been caused by the dates of your proposed visit, which coincides with the date of the National Eisteddfod, held this year at Rhyd-yr-Onnen. This little town is situate within my constabulary area, and I shall be personally responsible for the maintenance of law and order there for that week, not an inconsiderable responsibility, as you may very well imagine, when a town accustomed to accommodating four thousand souls finds itself constrained to cater for twenty thousand. I suggest, therefore, that instead of spending only a week with me, you will honour me with your company for at least a fortnight, the first week of which you will spend at the Eisteddfod as my guest. I shall be staying at the Golden Harp Hotel, where I have also provisionally booked a room for your good self. I sincerely hope you will be able to join me there, because then, with the turmoil of my daily duties ended, I shall have the consolation of a quiet evening chat with you, talking about old times. The second week will be spent, according to our usual practice, trying out new flies in old streams. Please do come."

Hopkyn smiled. *"I have looked forward with joyous expectancy . . . accustomed to accommodating four thousand souls . . . not an inconsiderable responsibility . . . with the turmoil of my daily duties ended . . ."* How difficult it is, he thought, to know a man by his letters. Was it Sheridan who said of Goldsmith that he wrote like an angel and spoke like Poor Poll ? My old Colonel, when he writes a letter, has a Victorian smoothness of phrase that is the direct opposite of his bluff, hearty, gruff way of speaking. What an odd mixture the Old Man is ! Bit my head off when I first met him in the desert. Wasn't really my fault that I was a day late reporting at his H.Q. Thought I'd never get on with him. But those three years in North Africa made us get to know and to like each other. And the more I got to know him, the more I liked him. Made me his adjutant when he had his full Colonelcy. Strange that both of us should join the police when the war ended. He got to the top in one bound . . . Chief Constable. I started at the very bottom, foot-slogging with the Metropolitan. He did his very best to persuade me to transfer to his area. Wonder if he pulled any strings to help me when I told him it was my ambition to get to the Yard ? Wouldn't put it past him, he's an astute old fellow. He'd go all out to help a friend, especially if he felt under an obligation to him. I suppose I did save his life when the tank went on fire, but it was only because I happened to be within arm's length of him. What time is it ? Another hour till lunch. I'll go down to the Eisteddfod.

He joined the crowd, listening to the chatter around him.

"*That last note of his was flat, I tell you, half a tone flat it was . . .*"

"*D'ye see that painting of the girl an' the cat ? Won the Gold Medal it did, so it must be pretty good. Couldn't see anything in it myself, though . . .*"

"*But the words don't rhyme, man ! I know that you South Walians can't say the sound proper, like us in North Wales. But that's no excuse in the National, man . . .*"

"*Of course he shouldn't stand down-stage when he made that long speech. No sense of grouping at all ! And the pace was far too slow . . .*"

Music, painting, poetry, drama . . . the Eisteddfod not only filled the town, it filled the air as well. Thank God I accepted the Chief's invitation, thought Hopkyn. I'd forgotten what the National was like, nearly forgotten that I was Welsh myself. To hell with London ! This is where I belong. Listen to them ! Critics, every one of them, but honest genuine critics, trying to get at the meaning of things, not trying to be clever. Sincere, not supercilious ; candid, not capricious ; intelligent, not the intelligentsia. These are my people. I'm glad I'm Welsh. I'm proud to be one of them.

I'm getting maudlin and sentimental, he said. It's that third pint. I'll have to walk it off. But is it sentimental ? If I stopped a thousand Englishmen in the Strand and asked each of them who won the Hawthorne Prize for poetry this year, how many of them could tell me ? I don't know myself. And how many of them would sit for half an hour in a hot pavilion, listening to a college professor adjudicating an epic poem ?

Last Tuesday, I saw it happen. The pavilion wasn't big enough to hold the crowd that wanted to get in. Every seat was filled, two thousand more stood at the back and along the sides, stood there for half an hour, alive with interest, listening to a detailed criticism of the Crown Poem. And when the winning bard was escorted to the stage, the whole audience stood up to cheer him, as if he'd

15

just won the Derby. Yesterday, all over Wales, his name was on everyone's lips. The Crown Bard of the National Eisteddfod. A national hero.

Today, there will be an even greater hero. It's Thursday, the big day of the Eisteddfod. It used to be called Lloyd George's day. Many people thought it was Ll.G. who drew the crowd. But it wasn't. It's the Chair Bard. Thursday is still the big day of the Eisteddfod.

"Ticket, sir ?"

Hopkyn had arrived at the Eisteddfod field. He produced his official pass, and entered.

From the pavilion, magnified by loud-speakers, came the strains of harp music. Hopkyn stood and listened. A party of singers, singing a different air, broke into the harp music. This *penillion* singing—with the harp playing the air, and voices singing the accompaniment—was uniquely Welsh. The music ceased, there came a burst of applause, and Hopkyn walked on.

A short, sturdy, stockily built gentleman in a dark suit passed him, smiled pleasantly, and wished him good day. Hopkyn returned the smile, and turned to look after him. Who was he ? I'm sure I've met him. Recognised the voice. Ah ! Yes, of course. The Archdruid, Leader of the Bards. Looked much more imposing in his bardic robes. What a commanding presence he had on the stage ! The ceremony of crowning the bard on Tuesday was one of the most impressive spectacles I've ever seen. How many bards were there in the procession ? At least a couple of hundred. I sat at the back of the pavilion. The doors had been shut, and every seat was full. Not even standing room. Suddenly, the two big doors at the back of the stage were flung open. Two buglers stood there, in gold and purple. At their call, the huge audience rose to its feet.

Then there entered, between the buglers, the Bardic Standard, a resplendent banner borne by four men in red. A spotlight played on its colours, making them glitter. Following the standard came the bards in their flowing robes, blue and green and white. The Swordbearer took up his position by the Bardic Chair set in the centre of the stage, and finally the Archdruid himself entered. A prayer was sung, the Bards joined in the responses, and the Archdruid declared the *gorsedd* open.

He introduced the three adjudicators to the audience, and the senior one of the three delivered a summary of their comments. Sly digs at some of the competitors brought chuckles, an occasional humorous aside relieved the tension. But on the whole it was a sober, serious, scholarly analysis of the poems submitted for the Crown. Each competitor had a pen-name. The poet who called himself *Mab y Pridd* (Son of the Soil) was declared the winner.

The Archdruid faced the audience, repeated the pen-name, and asked him to stand. Ten thousand pairs of eyes darted to and fro to locate him. He stood up. A young man, pale with nervousness. Two white-robed bards stepped down from the stage, accompanied by an attendant bearing a purple-red gown in which to invest him. They escorted him to the stage while the organ played "See the conquering hero comes." The Archdruid welcomed him with a smile, shook his hand, and the two whispered together while the audience stood up and cheered. The Bard stood, biting his lip, too excited to smile, in front of the Bardic Chair. A score of press-photographers crouched in front of him. Lights flashed. Every newspaper in Wales wanted his photograph.

The Swordbearer held aloft his massive sword. Four bards helped him to hold it above the young man's head. The blade was half unsheathed.

The Archdruid called for the first time :
"Is there Peace ?"
The whole audience responded :
"Peace !"
In a louder voice, he called for the second time :
"Is there Peace ?"
And the huge audience again replied :
"Peace !"

17

Then for the third and the last time, the Archdruid, in a still louder voice, demanded :

"Is there Peace ?"

And ten thousand throats roared the response :

"PEACE !"

"Then," said the Archdruid, "no let or hindrance having arisen, I declare, in the face of the sun, the eye of light, that Dyfed Owen, of Cwm Bach in the county of Merioneth, be proclaimed the Crown Poet of Wales for this year."

The young man sat in the Bardic Chair, and the Eisteddfod Crown was placed on his head. Other bards came to congratulate him in verse, the Crown Song was sung in his honour, a group of young girls curtsied and danced before him. The ceremony closed with the singing of *Hen Wlad fy Nhadau*, the Welsh national anthem.

Colourful, dignified, majestic—but at the same time warm and homely and intimate : well-planned and well-produced. Especially this year, commented Hopkyn. Usually, the Archdruid announced the name and address of the winning bard at the start of the ceremony ; this year, however, he had waited until the Bard was about to be crowned before announcing his name, and the slight change in the timing had added to the tension and the expectancy.

What time is it ? I mustn't be late for lunch. I wonder if the Chief's going to see the Chairing Ceremony this afternoon ? I doubt it. It will be exactly the same spectacle, minus the Crown, as the one he saw on Tuesday. He wriggled in his seat during most of it. The only time he can keep still for any length of time is when he's fishing.

3. The Empty Chair

It had been a good lunch. The beer had given Hopkyn an appetite, the salmon was beautifully cooked, the salad fresh and crisp. Hopkyn felt comfortably full, materially and spiritually at peace with all the world.

He snuggled deeper into the armchair. The Chief, in the armchair opposite, was already asleep. The Old Man had had a very busy morning. The Procession of Bards at eight o'clock had forced him to get up early in case the crowd got out of hand. The little glen where the Bards were holding their *Gorsedd* was a lovely setting for their meeting, but it was far too small to accommodate the crowd who wished to see and hear them. However, the arrangements had worked quite smoothly, much to the Chief's delight, until a sudden thunder shower sent bards and spectators scuttling for shelter beneath the trees.

When that spot of bother had been sorted out, there had come an urgent summons for assistance from the other end of the town. One of the many charabancs carrying day visitors to the Eisteddfod had broken a back axle. An ever-growing queue of cars and coaches was held up behind it. The only solution in such a narrow road was to break two gaps in the fence alongside and divert the traffic through the adjoining field until the charabanc could be removed. The farmer, though, had proved obstreperous. Who was going to repair the damage? The Chief sent for the Eisteddfod Treasurer. Together, they were able to persuade the farmer that he would be fully recompensed. Still another minor crisis had been averted.

The Old Man looks tired, said Hopkyn to himself. The week has been too much of a strain. A nap will do him good. I might as well join him. I'm feeling rather drowsy. It's that beer again.

He wriggled until the cushion at his back provided a

more comfortable support, put back his head, shut his eyes, and immediately opened them again.

"How long have I been asleep ?" demanded the Chief. "What time is it, Hopkyn ?"

"Nearly three o'clock."

"Good ! They'll have closed the pavilion doors at half-past two to prevent anyone going in during the Chairing Ceremony. But there'll be a hell of a rush when it's over. I'll have to be there. No hurry, though. They'll be another half-hour before they've finished with the Chairing. They're broadcasting the ceremony, Hopkyn. Switch on the radio. There it is by the window."

Hopkyn got up, turned the dial to Welsh Regional, and switched on.

"Are you interested in poetry, Chief ?" he asked as he resumed his seat.

The Chief snorted.

"Not a bit ! But everybody's interested in the Chair Bard of the Eisteddfod, man ! All Wales is listening-in at this moment."

"Yes, I was . . ."

"Sh ! Listen !"

Hopkyn listened, and saw with his mind's eye the spectacle that had gripped him on Tuesday—the big stage, the army of bards, the massive sword held above the winner's head, the colourful setting. Once again he heard the Archdruid's magnificent voice demanding Peace, the responses of the huge audience, felt the hushed tension of their excitement, the anxious whispering, the eager waiting for the name of the winning Bard.

For the third and the last time, the Archdruid cried : "Is there Peace ?"

And for the third and the last time, ten thousand throats, with a roar that blasted the microphone, shouted : "PEACE !"

And then—suddenly, abruptly—there was silence, utter absolute silence.

Hopkyn sat up.

The Chief swore.

"Dam the set ! What's gone wrong with it, Hopkyn ?"

Hopkyn got up and went to the window. He looked at the set. The dial was still lit. He bent down to listen. The set was still alive.

"Give it a good shake, Hopkyn !"

"Eh ?"

"Shake it, man ! That's what I always do at home. Always works."

Hopkyn chuckled.

"The set's all right, Chief. I can hear it humming. The fault's at the other end. Connection gone wrong, probably."

"Technical hitch, that's what they call it. Technical hitch be damned ! It always happens when . . ."

"Sh ! It's back again."

A voice, speaking with only partially suppressed excitement, was apologising for the interruption.

"I'm afraid," continued the voice from the set, "that the stage microphone has gone out of commission. Somebody must have tripped over the cable. I'm unable to see from here what's happened to the Chair Bard because there's a group of people bending over him. When the huge audience was shouting Peace in response to the Archdruid's final call, the Chair Bard appeared to collapse on to the Chair. Two of the stage officials ran to him as he fell, and one of them must have tripped over the cable and disconnected it. The audience is getting restive. Most of them are standing up, craning their heads to see what's happening on the stage. The Archdruid has stepped forward. Ah ! I can see the Bard now, he's still lying huddled on the Chair. The Archdruid is asking everybody to sit down and keep calm. While he is speaking, a man has run up the stairs on to the stage, and has knelt down by the Bard. The Archdruid is getting the crowd in hand : what a glorious voice he has, just what is needed at a time like this. They're obeying him, all sitting down, still excited of course, but quieter. The man who came on to the stage has stood up, and is speaking to the Archdruid. Oh, I know who he is now.

It's Doctor Lloyd, the local practitioner here. The Archdruid is nodding his head. Looks very serious. He's going to speak again. The doctor and another man are helping the Bard to his feet. No ! They're carrying him off the stage. The Archdruid lifts his hand for silence . . ."

"Come on, Hopkyn !" said the Chief. "I'll have to go there. If one hysterical woman screams now, she'll start a panic. And even the Archdruid won't be able to control ten thousand people in a panic. Come on !"

4. Doctor's Dilemma

The Chief, with a foot on the brake and a hand on the hooter, drove his little Austin as hard as he could through the crowded street.

"I'm frightened, Hopkyn," he muttered. "If the huge audience in that pavilion gets out of hand, God knows what might happen. Children trampled under foot, women crushed to death—blast that woman ! Why the devil did she want to dart into the road like that ? Right in front of me !"

Hopkyn chuckled. The Chief, absorbed in his fear of a panic in the pavilion, was himself creating a considerable panic in the street. The Amazon he had brushed against let out a piercing scream which drowned the noise of the hooter. She was a big woman with a loud voice. In a collision between her and the little car, thought Hopkyn, the Austin would come off second best.

The scream had helped to cleave a passage through the crowd, and the Chief took full advantage of it. Sudden bursts of speed alternating with abrupt halts at last brought them to the entrance to the Eisteddfod grounds. The constable on duty there recognised the Chief, opened the gate to admit the car, and saluted.

"Everything quiet, Hughes ?" barked the Chief.

"Yessir," replied Hughes. "They're singing."

"Good. I'll park the car here."

Hopkyn got out, and stood for a moment listening to the singing from the pavilion.

It was a Welsh hymn tune. He knew the tune, but couldn't at first recollect its name. He found himself humming it, and the name came to him. Of course, it was *Hyfrydol*. One of his favourites. What a wonderful tune it was ! He could remember . . .

"Come on, Hopkyn," said the Chief. "Don't stand mooning there. Let's see what's happening in the pavilion."

What's the hurry ? Hopkyn asked himself. Can't he hear what's happening ? They're singing. Music has calmed the troubled breast. Who said that ? Congreve, of course. "Music hath charms to soothe the savage breast." Savage, not troubled. But it's equally true of troubled breast, especially of us Welsh. The best singing I've ever heard was at the churchyard in my native village, at a funeral when they sang *O fryniau Caersalem* over the open grave. When our feelings are wrung, we Welsh break into song. "Our sweetest songs are those which tell of saddest thought." Emotional escapism ? Perhaps.

"I've just been ringing your hotel, sir," said the Sergeant standing at the stage door of the pavilion to the Chief. "They told me you were on the way here."

"Where have they taken him, Sergeant ?"

"Into the Secretary's Office, sir. Just off the stage. The doctor's with him."

"Right. I'll go and see him."

"This way, sir."

He led them through a narrow corridor flanked by small rooms used as offices. The corridor ended in a ramp that led up to the stage. At the foot of the ramp was a door with GENERAL SECRETARY painted on it. The Sergeant stopped at this door, and knocked.

A young man opened the door.

"Oh, it's you, Chief. Come in, please."

He held the door open for them. The Chief went in, and Hopkyn followed him. The Sergeant was half-way in when the young man stopped him.

"Will you guard the door, please, Sergeant?" he asked. "The doctor wants everybody kept out."

A look of disappointment fluttered over the Sergeant's face. But before he could reply, the Chief had turned round.

"That's right," said the Chief. "Stand in the corridor outside, Roberts, and don't let anybody in."

"Very well, sir."

The young man closed the door.

"I'm glad you've come," he told the Chief. "Things are rather serious here."

"Oh. What's wrong?"

"You've heard what has happened?"

"I was listening-in on the radio. I know that the Bard collapsed." The Chief paused, and looked into the young man's face. "Is he dead?"

The young man nodded.

"Yes," he said. "Heart attack. He was dead when the doctor and I carried him off the stage."

"How many people know he's dead?"

"Just the two of us—the doctor and me. Everybody else thought he'd fainted. Dr. Lloyd sent everybody out of here as soon as we brought the body in. When they'd gone, he told me he was dead. Nobody else knows. Except the doctor and me—and you two."

He looked, rather questioningly, at Hopkyn as he spoke. Hopkyn felt the question in his voice.

"Better introduce us, Chief," he suggested.

"Sorry," said the Chief. "This is Mr. John Phillips, the Eisteddfod Secretary. Detective Inspector Hopkyn, of Scotland Yard."

"A detective?"

Hopkyn smiled.

"Not at the moment, Mr. Phillips. Just an ordinary visitor to the Eisteddfod. I'm on holiday, and spending part of my leave with my friend the Chief Constable."

The singing in the pavilion had stopped. There came a strained silence. In the wall of the office, facing the audience, was a large glass panel with a thin lace curtain.

24

Anybody standing near the window could see into the auditorium without being seen by the audience. A smaller window, in the left-hand wall, looked out on the stage.

Hopkyn stepped to the big window, and looked at the audience. Now that the singing had ceased, they were getting restive. People turned in their seats to talk to one another, perturbed, nervous, uneasy.

Then came the Archdruid's voice.

"My friends," he said, "you sang *Hyfrydol* so beautifully that I am now going to ask you to sing another favourite of mine, the hymn-tune *Llef*, in my opinion the best tune ever written. Sing it with all your hearts ! Let the Bard hear you sing it ! It will give him a new strength and a new courage. And then we may be able to carry on with the Chairing Ceremony. Now, altogether—*O Iesu Mawr, rho'th anian bur.*"

The singing was resumed, and the audience once more settled down in their seats.

There came a knock at the door. Phillips went to open it. He and the Sergeant had a whispered colloquy in the corridor. Then he came back, shutting the door behind him.

"What shall I say ?" he asked. "The Archdruid has sent a messenger to ask how the Bard is."

"For God's sake," replied the Chief, "don't tell him he's dead ! Another shock following so close on the heels of the first one . . ."

"But we can't keep it quiet for long !" remonstrated the Secretary.

"Of course not. But this isn't the time to announce it. What do you think, Hopkyn ?"

"I suggest, Chief, that you ask the Archdruid to announce that the Chairing Ceremony must be postponed for today, but that a special announcement will be made later, as soon as the Committee has had an opportunity to talk things over with the doctor."

"Good. Will you write the message, Phillips ?"

"Better still," advised Hopkyn, "for Mr. Phillips to

25

speak himself with the Archdruid. He can tell him confidentially that things are rather serious, but that the Archdruid should make the announcement sound as if the ceremony was only being postponed. Do you think the Archdruid can do that ?" he asked Phillips.

The Secretary nodded.

"Yes," he said. "He's already saved the situation once. When the Bard collapsed, there could easily have been a panic here. I've never been so terrified in my life ! But the Archdruid kept calm, and he has such a magnificent voice that the audience had to listen to him. He told them what a strain the ceremony is for a young bard, and how he himself, when he was first crowned at the National, nearly fainted from excitement. He appealed to them to give the doctor a little time to attend to his patient—he went on talking, calmly and quietly, all the time the doctor and I were carrying out the body."

"Good. Go and have a talk with him while they're singing. We'll go and see the doctor, Hopkyn. I suppose there will have to be an inquest. Damn nuisance. Where's the body, Phillips ?"

"I have a small sitting-room at the back here. We carried him there because there's a couch in the room."

"Right. You go and see the Archdruid, Phillips. Then phone for an ambulance. Feeling better now ?"

"Much better, thanks. Been rather a shock, though."

"Of course it has. But you've got over the worst of it. See you later."

The Secretary went out, and the Sergeant shut the door behind him.

"Good man, Phillips," said the Chief. "Tip-top organiser. Woodwork master at the Modern School. But I'm afraid he's a bit too young for a big job like this. The strain is beginning to tell on him. Well, let's see the doctor about an inquest."

The door opened immediately to his knock.

"Come in, Chief," said the doctor. "Who's your companion ?"

"Detective Inspector Hopkyn, Scotland Yard."

"A detective ?"

Hopkyn smiled.

"Hasn't a detective—and a Welshman at that—the right to be at the Eisteddfod ? We're not always on duty, you know."

"Hopkyn was my adjutant in the army," explained the Chief. "He's spending part of his leave with me. You didn't think he was here on business, did you ?"

"I did," said the doctor, quietly and seriously.

Hopkyn glanced at him sharply.

"What do you mean ?" asked the Chief.

The doctor turned to look at the body lying on the couch behind him.

"You know he's dead ?" he asked.

The Chief nodded.

"His heart, wasn't it ?"

"Yes," replied Dr. Lloyd. "His heart. There's a bullet in it."

5. A Study in Red

The Chief looked at the doctor, aghast.

"A bullet ?" he repeated. "You're joking, doctor !"

"Do I look as if I were joking ?" asked Dr. Lloyd. "It would be in very poor taste if I did."

"But . . . Good heavens, man ! . . . you don't mean to tell me that the man was shot, with ten thousand people looking on ?"

"I was one of the ten thousand, Chief. I sat in the front row, right opposite the Bard. I saw him fall."

Hopkyn could contain himself no longer. He had no official right to interest himself in the affair, but at the same time he knew that the intimate friendship which existed between him and the Chief would justify what would otherwise appear officious.

"Doctor," he asked, "when you saw him fall, had you at that time any reason to believe that it was fatal ?"

Dr. Lloyd hesitated, and then shook his head.

"Not at the time," he replied.

"But you did realise that it was something more serious than an ordinary case of fainting ?"

"Yes," said Dr. Lloyd.

"Why ?" asked the Chief.

"I had been watching him rather carefully," explained the doctor. "Not because I'm interested in either poets or poetry, as such. But because it's always interesting to note a man's reaction at times of tension."

Hopkyn nodded.

"I felt the same way on Tuesday," he commented, "during the Crowning Ceremony. The spectacle was very well stage-managed, but all the time I found myself full of sympathy for the chief actor in it. The poor fellow looked so terribly uncomfortable—face twitching, hands gripping the arms of the chair—"

"Today's Bard," interrupted Dr. Lloyd, "showed no signs of nervousness. That's why he interested me. He was so different from Tuesday's winner. This one loved the whole show, smiled and posed and beamed through it all. And then, quite suddenly, as abruptly as a child wipes his slate clean with a wet rag, his smile disappeared. He was staring at somebody behind me—"

"Directly behind you ?" asked Hopkyn.

The doctor thought for a moment.

"I can't be exact," he replied slowly. "He was looking over my head at somebody who was certainly sitting behind me. I cannot say how far behind, nor how much to the right or to the left. I don't think it was anybody sitting in the row next to me. The impression I had was that it was somebody a few rows back."

The Chief coughed impatiently.

"He saw somebody sitting behind you, and it gave him a shock. Is that what happened ?"

"There are some people," said Dr. Lloyd, "who are not able, or at least make no effort, to hide their feelings. The Chair Bard was one of them. He was delighted with the show, loved being the centre-piece of it, and he made no

28

bones about expressing his pleasure. Then he saw somebody he knew. I could see the sudden glint of recognition in his eyes."

"Somebody he was afraid of ?" suggested Hopkyn.

"Somebody he was mortally afraid of," replied the doctor. "He was frightened. More than frightened. He had the look of a man who saw death staring at him."

Hopkyn looked hard at the doctor.

"You're quite sure about this, Dr. Lloyd ?"

"It made a very vivid impression on me."

"It certainly did," agreed Hopkyn. "But are you perhaps dramatising what happened in the light of later knowledge ?"

Dr. Lloyd smiled, shaking his head.

"I see your point," he said, "but . . . No, Inspector ! I'm not imagining things because I found out afterwards that he had been shot. I didn't know that he had been shot until we brought him into this room. But I knew—even before he collapsed on the stage—that he had had a shock, and a very severe shock."

"And you thought at the time that the collapse was due to the shock ?"

"I did."

"Did the collapse follow immediately on the shock ? Or was there an interval between them ?"

"A few seconds only. He gasped suddenly, clutched at his heart with both hands, and collapsed. Some of the people sitting near me shouted that he had fainted. They hadn't noticed what I had seen. I knew it was more serious than a faint."

"A heart attack ?"

"To me, it looked like angina. I ran up the stairs on to the stage. As soon as I saw his face, I knew that he was dead."

"But you didn't know at that time that he had been shot ?"

"No. I told the Archdruid to keep the crowd quiet—most of them had jumped to their feet when the Bard collapsed—and the Secretary and I carried the body in here."

"You didn't tell the Archdruid that he was dead ?"

"No. The crowd was already over-excited."

"Excellent, doctor !" exclaimed the Chief. "Thank God you kept it quiet !"

"What happened afterwards ?" asked Hopkyn.

"A crowd of officials followed us into the office," said the doctor, "so we brought the body in here, and put it on the couch in that corner. Then I told Phillips to clear the people out of the office and ask Sergeant Roberts to stay in the corridor and stop anyone coming in. Phillips went, and I examined the body. It was then that I found he had been shot. The bullet has gone too deep for me to get it out without my instruments, but I can show you where it went in. Just below the heart."

Dr. Lloyd went to the couch, and bent over the body of the young man stretched out on it.

He was in his middle twenties, clean-shaven except for a thin line of moustache arching his upper lip like a plucked eyebrow. His hair was jet black, brushed back diagonally from a centre parting. High cheek-bones, a long thin nose, rather a weak chin. A trace of incipient bagginess beneath the eyes. Even in death, he looked rather precious and effeminate.

Looks more like a gigolo than a bard, mused Hopkyn, looking down at him. But poetry is a flower that blooms in strange places. Wasn't it Oscar Wilde who walked down the Strand with a lily in his hand ?

Dr. Lloyd opened the purple-red robe in which the Bard had been invested before being escorted to the stage. Underneath the robe, he wore a tweed sports-coat and a flowered shirt. The coat hung open, and the shirt was unbuttoned. The doctor folded back the shirt, and pointed to the bullet hole below the heart.

"You can see that it didn't bleed very much," he said. "The bullet went straight into the heart, and as soon as the heart stopped pumping, the circulation ceased. What blood that did flow soaked through the shirt into the coat.

Very little blood could come through this thick tweed. Even if some of the blood did soak through, it wouldn't be very noticeable on a robe of this colour."

Hopkyn nodded.

"Very lucky for the murderer," he commented, "or a very carefully planned murder. May I have another look at the bullet hole, doctor ?"

The blood had been wiped off. It was a very small hole. Strange that death had entered by so small a hole.

"When can you get the bullet out ?" Hopkyn asked.

"As soon as I get him to the mortuary," replied the doctor. "It's probably still embedded in the heart.'

"And the calibre ?" asked Hopkyn.

"I can't be absolutely certain until I get the bullet out, but it looks like a .22."

Hopkyn nodded.

"Yes," he agreed. "And a .22 can be fired from either a rifle or a revolver. If a rifle was used, anybody sitting inside the pavilion could have fired the shot, or even somebody standing just outside. He was well within range of a rifle. I don't envy you the job of finding a murderer among ten or twelve thousand suspects, Chief."

The Chief chuckled, dryly.

"You needn't envy me," heretorted. "I'm handing the case over to you."

"You can't," objected Hopkyn. "I'm on leave."

"You won't be," grinned the Chief, "as soon as I get on the 'phone to the Assistant Commissioner. You don't imagine, do you, that the Yard would send another man here when you're already on the spot ?"

"All right, Chief. You win. I'll take over. You'll give me a free hand ?"

"There's an old Welsh proverb, my lad, which tells us not to do the barking ourselves if we keep a dog. You can do what you like provided you keep me in the picture."

There came a knock at the door. Hopkyn hurriedly covered the corpse with its purple robe, and turned to see who was coming in.

It was Phillips, the Secretary.

"The ambulance has arrived," reported Phillips. "Shall I tell the men to come in ?"

Dr. Lloyd looked at Hopkyn, and Hopkyn nodded.

"Yes," said the doctor. "Get them to reverse the van as near the stage door as possible. We'll get him out as quietly as we can. Will you be coming with us, Inspector ?"

Hopkyn shook his head.

"The Chief and I will follow you later," he replied. "We'll get things straightened out here first."

"Right !" said the doctor. "Tell the men to come in, Phillips."

It took only a few minutes to put the body on a stretcher, and carry it out into the ambulance waiting outside. The doctor brushed off a group of curious newspaper men who were prowling outside the door, and jumped into the van.

The Chair Bard, still dressed in his purple robe, was on his way to the mortuary.

Hopkyn, the Chief, and Phillips sat in the office. The Chief was writing in his notebook. Phillips had lit a cigarette and was pulling at it nervously.

Hopkyn took out his pipe, and filled it slowly. The Chief was right, he said to himself : Phillips is too inexperienced for a job like this. The strain is wearing him down. Shall I tell him now about the murder, that the Bard was shot ? Better not. We don't want another collapse. What about the other Eisteddfod officials ? The Chairman of the Committee is probably an older man. More experienced.

"Mr. Phillips," he said, "I think you should call a meeting of your Committee as soon as you can. What's the procedure ?"

"You mean the Executive Committee ?"

"I suppose so. How many members are there on it ?" "Sixty four."

"Good heavens ! As many as that ?"

"We've got a dozen sub-committees, you see, and all

the officials of the sub-committees are members of the Executive Committee. There are . . ."

"Surely," said Hopkyn, "there's no need to call all these people together to decide on a matter of emergency. Isn't there a smaller committee with authority to act ?"

"The Chairman and the Treasurer and myself have been given full authority to take emergency measures . . ."

"Good ! How long will it take you to get them together ?"

"They're on the stage," said Phillips. "I'll go and get them . . ."

Hopkyn stopped him.

"Just a minute, Phillips. Now that the people are quiet, we must be careful not to disturb them. If you appeared suddenly on the stage, and they saw you and the other two officials as suddenly leave it, they'd start imagining things. Leave well alone."

"That's right," said the Chief. "There's no immediate hurry for a meeting, is there, Hopkyn ?"

"No," replied Hopkyn. "We'll go along to the hospital and have a word with the doctor, Chief. Could you and the others follow us there, Phillips, in about half an hour?"

The Secretary was obviously on tenterhooks. Hopkyn felt extremely sorry for him. Organising a huge festival like the National Eisteddfod had meant hard work. Phillips had been at it without much respite for two years. The last three months had been a terrific strain, and the sudden death of the Chair Bard had looked like being the last straw.

"Look here, Phillips," said Hopkyn, "this is the first time you've organised a big job like this. It's the biggest thing you've ever done, and everybody agrees that you've made a very good job of it. The success of the Eisteddfod is a feather in your cap. Don't spoil it now by losing control. What happened today is none of your fault, you couldn't have foreseen it, and you could have done nothing to prevent it. But now that it has happened, you can do a lot to retrieve the situation. If you lose your head now, all the good work you have done for the last two years will

33

go by the board. Pull yourself together, man ! Everything is working smoothly. The Archdruid has got the crowd well in hand, and the Eisteddfod can now go on as if nothing had happened. The people are naturally disappointed because the Chairing Ceremony was interrupted, but even that gave them an unexpected thrill, and they've got over it. All you need do now is to carry on normally. Wait here until the bards have left the stage, and when the choir competition begins, get hold of the Chairman and the Treasurer and bring them along to the hospital. Tell them that we want a word with them. Is that clear ?"

Phillips had listened attentively to Hopkyn's homily.

"Thank you, Inspector," he said. "That has done me a lot of good." He smiled, rather wanly. "I was in need of a mental shaking. I could feel myself getting panicky."

"No need to apologise, lad," put in the Chief. "Older men than you have lost their heads in a crisis. But as far as the audience is concerned, all that's happened is that the Chair Bard has been taken ill, and that you've had to postpone the Chairing. They don't know he's dead. They'll have to be told, of course, and we'll have to decide on the best time to break the news. That's up to you and the other officials. Can you get them to the hospital in half an hour ?"

"Yes. Should I tell them that the Bard is dead ?"

The Chief looked at Hopkyn, who shook his head.

"No," he said. "Just tell them that things are more serious than the Archdruid gave out, and that the doctor wants to see them at the hospital."

"But if they start questioning me . . ." began Phillips.

"Look here," interrupted Hopkyn. "The best thing for you to do is to get your clerk to give them the message, and for you to come along with us in the Chief's car. We'll drop you at The Golden Harp. Do you drink ?"

"Very seldom."

"All the better. A large whisky will do you all the more good. The private lounge will be empty at this time of day. Sit there quietly on your own for half an hour,

drink your whisky, and come along to the hospital.
Right ?"

Phillips nodded.

"Right, Inspector. I'll follow your prescription."

"Good. We'll get going then. Ready, Chief ?"

6. Official Announcement

The Chairman of the Eisteddfod Committee was William
Rowlands the Ironmonger.

All the shops in Rhyd-yr-Onnen followed the Victorian
custom of calling themselves "Houses". There was a
London House, a Manchester House, a Bristol House,
even a Paris House. Edward Rowlands, William's
father, went further afield when he named his shop
Universal Stores.

The business was built on sound conservative lines. It
catered mostly for the outlying villages, and was a very
busy place on market days. His farmer customers seldom
paid for anything in cash, and William had to wait a
long while for his money. This credit system, however,
helped to retain old customers, which was a very good
thing for William, who had neither the gumption nor the
acumen to expand the business.

William was a talker, not a doer. He was a big, heavily
built man with a loud booming voice that forced people
to listen to him. As he took advantage of every opportunity to get up and speak, people had to listen to him very
often. He could speak for hours on any topic without
saying anything new or original about it. Had he anything to say that was worth listening to, William could
have been the Demosthenes of Wales.

Everybody was surprised when William was elected
Chairman of the Eisteddfod Executive Committee.
Everybody except William. William was astute, and had
played his cards very cunningly.

When the idea of inviting the National Eisteddfod

35

to Rhyd-yr-Onnen was first mooted, William was Chairman of the Rhyd-yr-Onnen Urban District Council. He had been elected to that office merely because he happened to be the senior member of the Council. The Chair was filled in order of seniority, and William automatically stepped into it when his turn came.

He was so big that he overflowed it. Indeed, it may have been a feeling of physical frustration which fired in William an ambition to fill a bigger Chair. He saw his opportunity when he heard that there was a movement afoot to invite the National Eisteddfod to Rhyd-yr-Onnen. For just that one week, Rhyd-yr-Onnen would be the Capital of Wales. If he pulled the right strings, William could be—for that one week—the uncrowned King of Wales.

The idea of getting the Eisteddfod to Rhyd-yr-Onnen was not his. William would never have thought of it. Nor did the idea originate with any of his fellow-members on the Urban District Council. They were as unimaginative as he. It was a young Methodist minister who first thought of it. He was a poet, and had won a couple of chairs at smaller eisteddfodau. He wrote a letter to the *County Herald* suggesting that representatives of the various literary Societies in the town (every Chapel had its own Literary Society) should meet to discuss the possibility of inviting the Royal National Eisteddfod of Wales to Rhyd-yr-Onnen in 1951. He quoted precedents, and reminded his readers how successful the National had been when it visited small towns like Rhyd-yr-Onnen, such as Dolgellau, Llandybie, Fishguard and Denbigh. The Eisteddfod, he argued, is too big a venture for a small village ; on the other hand, it gets lost in big towns like Cardiff and Swansea. The ideal venue is a small town. Furthermore, Rhyd-yr-Onnen was ideally situated geographically to be the cultural Mecca of Wales for the first week in August. He appealed to the Rhyd-yr-Onnen Urban District Council to give the project its official support.

William saw his opportunity, and pounced. As

Chairman of the Council, he presided at the public meeting called to discuss the suggestion. The meeting was well attended. Lovers of the Eisteddfod from all the outlying villages came there to pledge their support. A small committee was formed to draw up a petition to the Eisteddfod National Council, the body which decides every year where the Eisteddfod will be held. William automatically became Chairman of the Petition Committee.

The National Eisteddfod Council accepted Rhyd-yr-Onnen's invitation, and for a month afterwards Rhyd-yr-Onnen became committee mad. The National Eisteddfod is so famous a festival that everybody was eager to serve on one or more of its many committees. Music, Poetry, Drama, Arts, Handicrafts, First Aid, Brass Bands, etc.—there was a special committee for every section, each presided over by its own Chairman. So many Chairmen were elected for so many committees that the only one left for the Executive Committee was William himself. It was the survival of the unfittest.

So much for William. The Treasurer of the Eisteddfod Executive Committee was Mr. Price Jenkins, a horse of a very different colour. Chronologically, he and William were of the same age, in the early sixties. Physically, he was half the size of William. Intellectually, they were aeons apart.

Jenkins was a retired Bank Manager, and in more respects than one resembled the late Sir Stafford Cripps. While the Chairman beamed and boomed, the Treasurer sat quietly thinking. When William soared and swelled more than usual, Jenkins would ask a short question, sharp and incisive. It was like pricking a balloon, but done so adroitly that the balloon itself never felt the prick. When it happened, and it happened very often in committee, William found himself wondering how and when and why he had sat down.

Phillips, the Secretary, stood at the window of the Matron's room at the Hospital, looking at the two of them coming up the drive to the main entrance. William, as

37

usual, was talking and gesticulating as he walked.
Jenkins, as usual, did not appear to be listening to him.

As they passed the window, William saw the Secretary
and waved to him. He waved as if he hadn't seen Phillips
for years. He clutched at the Treasurer's arm, and
pointed to the window. Jenkins turned his head, saw
Phillips, and nodded to him. William hesitated a moment,
waved again at Phillips, and trotted after the Treasurer,
still talking.

Phillips turned to the Chief Constable.

"They've come. Shall I show them in ?"

"Yes, please," replied the Chief. "We won't wait for
Inspector Hopkyn. He and the doctor are busy with the
body."

Phillips left the room, leaving the door open behind
him. William and Jenkins had just come into the Hall.
He motioned to them, and just as William was going to
speak, signalled to him to be quiet. William stared at him
open-mouthed, stopped dead for a moment, remembered
he was in a hospital, and then lumbered after Phillips
like an elephant with sore feet, in a grotesque effort not
to make a noise. Jenkins followed them into the room,
closed the door behind him, and stood there looking
questioningly at the Chief.

There was no need for introductions. The Chief
Constable had already met the Eisteddfod officials, and
had taken an immediate dislike to the Chairman. Being
himself a man of few words, the Chief hated verbal
pomposity in others. He liked and respected the Treasurer,
and it was Jenkins whom he now addressed by name.

"Good day, Mr. Jenkins. Sit down, both of you. I've
got something to tell you."

Jenkins sat down by the table, without speaking.
William shook his head ponderously, coughed sympathetically, shook his head again, and asked in a funereal
tone,

"About the Chair Bard, I presume ? Dear, dear !
Poor fellow, poor fellow ! The excitement was too much

for him. And how is he now ? It was about him you wished to speak to us, was it not ?"

"Yes," said the Chief curtly. "Sit down."

William, still shaking his head, sat down.

"You have been told," continued the Chief, "that things are more serious than the Archdruid announced."

It was not a question, but William took it as a cue. The Chief cut him short with two words.

"He's dead."

What William was going to say rattled in his throat. The shock was so great that words failed him. His chin sagged. Phillips, looking at him, was suddenly tempted to laugh.

"Heart attack ?"

It was Jenkins who asked the question. The news of the Bard's death had left Jenkins unruffled.

"Dead !" William had at last assimilated the fact, and had got up on his big feet. "Dead ! Struck down at the height of his fame, in the hour of his glory, with the cheers of the multitude ringing in his ears ! In the midst of life, we are in death ! What a terrible calamity ! Ten thousand people looking on, and unbeknown to us all, a lonely soul starting on its long journey into the dark. My friends, what can we say, what can we do, in the face of such a tragedy as this ?"

He took a deep breath, and Jenkins answered his question.

"You can sit down."

William sat. Without looking at him, Jenkins fired another question at the Chief.

"I asked you if it was a heart attack. Was it ?"

"No. He was shot. Murdered."

There was a short, strained silence. William was staring uncomprehendingly at the Chief, mouth open, eyes blank, too dazed to think. Jenkins, elbow on table, was meditatively stroking his chin with his hand.

The Chief looked at them both, and a strange thought crossed his mind.

I wonder, he asked himself, if these two know anything

about it ? One looks so shocked that he seems to be over-acting the part, and the other has taken it so calmly that he might be expecting something of the sort.

Mr. Price Jenkins was certainly taking it very calmly indeed. He was now taking a cigarette out of his case, and tapping one end of it against his thumbnail. The metallic click of the case as he shut it made William jump.

"Murdered !" gasped William. The tremor in his voice made his whole body quake. "The Chair Bard of the Royal National Eisteddfod of Wales murdered on the stage ! It is incredible ! I refuse to believe it ! It's . . . it's . . ."

For the second time in his life, William was at a loss for words.

The Treasurer turned a cool gaze on Phillips, who was still standing by the window.

"Phillips," he asked, "did you know about this ?"

"Not until the Chief Constable told me a few minutes ago."

"You didn't know he had been shot when you helped to carry him off the stage ?"

"No, I didn't even know he was dead until Dr. Lloyd told me."

"When you wrote me that note, half an hour ago, you knew he was dead ?"

William recovered his voice. This was something he could grasp. If the Secretary was to be reprimanded for a breach of duty, it was his privilege as Chairman, not the Treasurer's, to rebuke him.

"Phillips," he boomed, "I am surprised—indeed, I am astounded—that you saw fit to conceal the knowledge from the Chairman of your committee. What will people think of us when they discover that we allowed the body of the dead Bard to be . . ."

Once again, the Treasurer interrupted him, quietly and incisively.

"You did quite right, Phillips. I congratulate you. Death was instantaneous ?"

"The doctor said he had been shot through the heart,"

put in the Chief. "Nobody could have done anything to save his life."

"I ran to him as soon as I saw him fall." There was still a tremor in the Secretary's voice. "I thought he had fainted. Then Doctor Lloyd came, and examined him. He said something to the Archdruid, and asked me to help him carry the . . . the body. But I didn't know then that he was dead, not until we had taken him through the office into the little sitting-room. The doctor asked me to send everybody out of the office, and when I came back he told me the Bard was dead."

"He told nobody else ?" asked Jenkins.

"No."

"So nobody knows of the death except us four and the doctor . . . and the Matron, of course ?"

"And Detective Inspector Hopkyn."

"Who ?" The Treasurer turned a puzzled face to the Chief Constable. "Who is Detective Inspector Hopkyn ?"

"He's a friend of mine," replied the Chief. "He's on leave from Scotland Yard, and spending part of his holiday as my guest. I've asked him to take over the case."

William had been struggling hard to keep up with the conversation. The situation was getting beyond him. But the mention of Scotland Yard brought him to earth. This was a real murder they were talking about, just like those in the *News of the World*.

"A detective from Scotland Yard !" he repeated. "Here in Rhyd-yr-Onnen ?"

"Very lucky for us he is," said the Chief curtly. "Inspector Hopkyn is one of the very best men they've got. If anybody can solve this murder, he can."

"You are sure it is murder ?" asked the Treasurer.

"He couldn't have shot himself, could he ?"

"I was not thinking of suicide," said the Treasurer. "What I had in mind was manslaughter."

The Chief stared at him, puzzled.

"An accident, you mean ?"

Jenkins did not reply for a moment. He pulled steadily

at his cigarette, weighing his words carefully as he spoke.

"A man is shot. It may be suicide, manslaughter, or murder. In this instance, we can rule out suicide. He couldn't have shot himself without being seen doing it. So it must be either murder or manslaughter. If the bullet was intended for him, it was murder. But if the man with the gun intended the bullet for somebody else, and shot the Bard by mistake, it could be manslaughter."

He spoke as impersonally as a college professor explaining a theorem in Euclid. The Chief looked at him with surprise.

"Good gracious !" he said. "What the devil made you think of manslaughter ?"

"It's part of my training," replied Jenkins. "In the Bank, when I was approached for a loan or an overdraft, I had to weigh up all the possibilities. I've got into the habit of analysing a situation."

The Chief smiled.

"You and Hopkyn should get on well together," he remarked. "And unless I'm mistaken, here he is."

Hopkyn came in alone. Dr. Lloyd had completed the post-mortem and had gone home. The Chief introduced Hopkyn to the two Eisteddfod officials, and then added,

"Mr. Jenkins was asking me when you came in, Hopkyn, if we're certain it is murder, not manslaughter."

Hopkyn turned to the Treasurer.

"You mean, Mr. Jenkins, that the wrong man was shot ?"

Jenkins nodded.

"There were a number of people around him when he was shot," continued Hopkyn. "The Archdruid stood on his left, the Gorsedd Recorder on his right. There were several other bards holding up the sword above his head. Is that what you had in mind, Mr. Jenkins ?"

"Yes."

William felt his heart give a thump inside him. He had suddenly realised that he himself was on the stage at the time of the shooting, and that never before had he been so near to sudden death.

42

"This is terrible !" he gasped. "A man shooting indiscriminately at the stage could have killed any one of us ! I was sitting only a few yards away !"

Hopkyn tried not to laugh. And then, as suddenly as it had occurred to the Chief a few minutes previously, the same thought crossed his mind also. Was the Chairman such a fool as he seemed ? Or was he putting on an act ?

"Mr. Rowlands," he asked, "where were you when the Bard was shot ?"

"I was sitting at the table on the right hand side of the stage," replied William, very much perturbed. "Only a few yards away !"

"To the right of the Bard ?"

"Yes. Mr. Jenkins here was sitting beside me. We were watching the ceremony." William drew a deep breath. "And to think that . . ."

Jenkins cut across him.

"We both sat at the same table, Inspector, and the table was on the right hand side of the stage, facing the audience. Why do you ask ?"

"You want a plain answer, Mr. Jenkins ?"

"Please."

Hopkyn smiled.

"You realise, of course, that anybody within shooting distance of the murdered man can come under suspicion. You and Mr. Rowlands were only a few yards away when he was shot . . ."

"What !" gasped William. "You don't suspect Mr. Jenkins or me of shooting him ?"

"No," smiled Hopkyn. "I can acquit both of you. You were sitting to his right. He was shot in the heart. You two couldn't have done it from where you sat."

"Thank God !" sighed William.

"The bullet was not fired by anybody on the stage," continued Hopkyn. "The Bard was standing so much down stage that all the people on the stage were either beside him or behind him. The bullet came from the front. It entered the body about an inch below the heart, pierced the left ventricle, and was embedded in the

43

upper vertebrae. If, at the time he was shot, the Bard was facing square to the audience, he was shot by somebody in front of him, a little to his left. If he were at the time turning slightly to the left, the bullet came from a wider angle to the left, but still from in front, not from the side. If he were turning slightly to the right, the bullet came from directly in front."

Jenkins nodded. Of the four listeners, he seemed to be the only one to see the full implication of what Hopkyn had said.

"I might be able to help you, Inspector," he suggested. "As Treasurer of the Eisteddfod, I had a large-scale plan made of the whole auditorium. Every seat is marked on the plan, except the benches at the far end. The plan might assist you to trace the murderer, or at least to find where the bullet might have come from."

"I shall be glad of a copy," replied Hopkyn, "but I'm afraid it won't help me very much just now. What is the seating capacity of the pavilion ?"

"Just over eight thousand."

"And the standing room ? How many more had pushed their way in ?"

"I should think about two thousand."

"The side-walls and the back-wall are shuttered, and all the shutters were open, were they not ?"

"Yes."

"There was a crowd at every shutter, looking in. Say another two thousand. That makes twelve thousand in all. If I shaded the plan to show where the bullet could have come from, and if the shaded part were only a tenth of the whole surface area of the pavilion, I'd still have twelve hundred suspects. The plan would have proved exceedingly useful, Mr. Jenkins, if the murder had been committed in a small pavilion with every seat numbered and reserved. We could then have located the murderer without much difficulty. But I'm afraid it won't help us very much in this case."

Jenkins again nodded.

"Yes," he agreed. "I quite understand, Inspector. But if you do need a copy, let me know."

"Thank you. I'll bear it in mind. It was very good of you to suggest it. Have you any other suggestion to make ?"

Jenkins smiled coldly.

"You haven't yet replied to my first one, Inspector. Are you absolutely sure it was murder, not manslaughter ?"

Hopkyn refused to be drawn.

"It's too soon to arrive at any conclusion," he hedged. "What I'm doing now is to collect evidence. The doctor has got the bullet out, and we'll send it off tonight for expert examination. Where's the nearest forensic laboratory, Chief ?"

"Preston. They'll get it tomorrow, and I'll ask them to telephone their report."

The Chief was growing impatient. He wanted to bring the interview to an end. He felt that Jenkins was interfering too much. It wasn't the Treasurer's business to find the murderer. That was Hopkyn's job. The business now in hand was to decide what official announcement to make.

He cleared his throat peremptorily.

"The man's dead. That's all we know at the moment. How he was shot and who shot him will come out later. Detective Inspector Hopkyn will see to that. What we've got to do now is to prepare an official announcement of the death. What are you going to tell the people, and when are you going to tell them ?"

William, who had been unusually silent for some time, got up on his feet.

"As Chairman of the Eisteddfod Executive Committee," he began, "it will be my painful duty to acquaint the audience of this terrible calamity. I shall . . ."

"No," said Jenkins.

William stopped abruptly, and looked down at him.

"If you mean that you're going back to the pavilion to tell the crowd that the Chair Bard has been shot dead," said Jenkins, "forget it. We've spent fifty thousand pounds on this Eisteddfod. If the story goes about that there's a fellow with a gun going around shooting people, the pavilion will be half empty tomorrow and Saturday. We've got to keep the shooting quiet until the Eisteddfod is over."

"But, man alive !" protested William, "you can't conceal a murder !"

"We don't know yet if it is a murder," retorted Jenkins. "Legally, we'll have to wait for an inquest before we can announce the cause of death. Am I right, Chief Constable ?"

"Not quite," growled the Chief. "But right or wrong, I'm not letting out anything about the shooting. Understand ?"

He snarled so fiercely at the Chairman that William felt in imminent danger of arrest.

"But . . . but . . ." he stammered, "we must tell the people something !"

The Chief, still scowling, turned to Jenkins.

"You're afraid that people will keep away from the Eisteddfod if they hear of the murder," he said. "I doubt it. They'd probably flock here in bigger crowds than ever to see the spot. That's what they usually do. I don't want a crowd of morbid sightseers here. I endorse your suggestion of keeping quiet about the cause of death until an inquest is held. We can use the inquest as an excuse, at least. What do you suggest, Hopkyn ?"

"I agree, Chief. All that need be done now is to announce the death. You could add that an inquest is to be held to ascertain the cause of death, and leave it at that. The less said the better."

"Personally," commented Jenkins, "I doubt very much whether we should make any announcement at all this afternoon. Telling an audience of ten thousand people, already over-excited, that they've seen a man dying on the stage would give them another nasty shock."

"Of course it would," agreed the Chief. "Damn silly thing to do ! Just the thing to cause a panic."

"So why not let the afternoon session carry on as if nothing had happened ?" suggested Jenkins. "Let the crowd disperse, and then, when the Eisteddfod session is over, we could let the news of the death leak out before the evening concert begins. The news would pass swiftly from mouth to mouth, and everybody would get to hear it. But it would have spread too slowly through the town to cause a panic."

"An excellent suggestion !" pronounced the Chief. "Just what should be done. No official announcement at all."

"We shall have to make some announcement at the evening concert," said Jenkins. "People will expect one. But it can be done quietly and decorously, and I know the very man to do it."

William coughed, and again got on his feet.

"I can assure you," he began, "that I shall pay a very moving tribute to the young man who was so suddenly taken from us. I shall . . ."

The cool voice of Jenkins again interrupted him.

"The man I have in mind," said he, "and the only one we can trust to do it with decorum and dignity, is the Archdruid."

William abruptly sat down.

"The very man !" said the Chief. "Phillips, will you get in touch with him ? Don't mention anything about the shooting, of course. Just tell him that the Bard is dead, and that an inquest will be held later to ascertain the cause of death. That's all. Right ?"

"I'll contact him immediately. Will you all excuse me, please ?"

Phillips left, and the Chief looked at William.

"Are you married, Mr. Rowlands ?"

William looked up with a start.

"Yes, yes."

"Don't tell your wife about the shooting, mind. Don't tell any of your friends about it. Not a word to anybody ! If I hear the slightest whisper is going round the town, I

47

shall make it my business to find out who started it. Understand ?"

William nodded, without a word.

"No need to warn you, Mr. Jenkins," said the Chief. "You realise the importance of keeping it quiet. And now, gentlemen, I'll bid you good afternoon. Inspector Hopkyn and I have some work to do."

7. Internal Evidence

When the door closed behind the Eisteddfod officials, Hopkyn turned to the Chief with a laugh.

"You sped the parting guests very abruptly, Chief."

"That big elephant of a Chairman was getting on my nerves," growled the Chief. "Jenkins also is a bit of a busybody." He paused a moment. "Anything in his suggestion of manslaughter, do you think ?"

Hopkyn shook his head.

"It's a remote possibility, of course. The man standing nearest the Bard was the Archdruid, but there was at least a yard separating them. Whoever fired the bullet would have to be standing a long distance away to make as wide a miss as that."

"He might be a very poor shot."

"In that case, he wouldn't have used a gun. No murderer uses a gun unless he feels pretty certain of getting his man. If he's a poor shot, he either gets close enough to the target to make sure of hitting it, or uses some other method of killing him."

"Bullet tell you anything ?"

"Not much. Here it is."

Hopkyn carefully unwrapped the piece of rag. The Chief looked at the bullet, and shook his head.

"Doesn't even look like a bullet," he remarked. "Knocked out of shape by the bone, I suppose ?"

Hopkyn nodded.

"Yes. That's the worst of these small bullets. When

you do get them out, they have so very little to tell you. A bigger bullet is much more communicative. It's big enough to hold its own in a collision."

"I'll send this to Preston tonight. The laboratory boys there may find something for you. They're pretty clever at this sort of thing."

"I know, Chief. But I'm afraid they won't be able to tell us very much about this one, beyond the fact that it's a .22."

"They might tell you what kind of a weapon it was fired from."

"Perhaps. It could have been fired from three different types—a rifle, a revolver, or an automatic. If it came from a rifle, the murderer could have been sitting as far from the stage as the back row of benches. He could even have been standing outside the pavilion, looking in through one of the shutters."

"Surely, Hopkyn, somebody or other would have noticed a man with a rifle ?"

"There was a sudden thunder shower this morning. And though we haven't had a drop of rain since then, most of the day visitors to the Eisteddfod brought rain-coats with them. A man standing outside the pavilion could have draped his coat over the rifle to hide it."

"The people standing beside him would have heard the shot, though."

"If he used a silencer ? And with twelve thousand people shouting at the top of their voices ?"

"Mmm," mumbled the Chief. "Might be possible, perhaps. But I don't see how he could take aim as carefully as he did if the rifle were draped in a coat."

"I agree, Chief. It's as remote a possibility as the Treasurer's suggestion of manslaughter."

"Far-fetched, both of them. Must have been a revolver, Hopkyn."

"I doubt it."

"Must have been ! And that makes your job a damn sight easier !"

The Chief had had a brainwave.

"Think of it, Hopkyn ! The fellow had to get as close as he could to the stage to make sure of his kill. That plan of Jenkins will come in very useful after all. All those front seats were numbered and reserved. We can find out who was sitting in them within . . . er . . . tell me, what's the maximum killing distance of a .22 revolver ?"

"I doubt whether you could kill a rabbit with it at twenty paces."

"Eh ?"

"The velocity is too low, Chief. The murderer may or may not have used a rifle, but I'm certain he didn't use a revolver."

"Oh." The Chief slowly wrapped the bullet in its rag, and put it in his waistcoat pocket. "What the devil did he use ?"

"It's used much more on the Continent than in this country, though I've come across it here once or twice, usually by a crook who draws the line at murder, and shoots to wound rather than to kill. It's a very accurate weapon, Chief—a high velocity automatic with a rifled barrel, about eight inches long, short enough to carry in a shoulder strap, and yet long enough to kill a man up to fifty yards. I doubt whether the Preston boys can tell from the marks of the rifling on the bullet whether it came from a rifle or an automatic. But you could ask them. And you could also check the maximum killing distance : I think it's lethal up to about fifty yards. In the meantime, there's some more internal evidence which I can study for myself."

"Eh ? What else did the doctor find inside him, Hopkyn ?"

Hopkyn laughed.

"I didn't mean that kind of internal evidence," he replied. "What I'm after is a copy of the prize poem."

The Chief stared at him in surprise.

"The prize poem ?" he repeated.

"Have you realised, Chief," asked Hopkyn, "that we've slipped up badly on this murder ? You know the book of rules. What's the very first thing to do in a case of murder ?"

"Ascertain the identity of the corpse."

"Do we know who this one is ?"

"Of course we do. The Chair Bard."

"What's his name ?"

"Eh ?"

Hopkyn chuckled.

"We don't know, Chief. The only thing we know about him is that he won the Chair. He was shot before the Archdruid could tell us his name."

"Well I'm damned !" The Chief looked it. "Never thought of it !" He brightened up again. "But his picture will be in all the papers tomorrow. We'll soon find out who he is."

"No need to wait until tomorrow," said Hopkyn. "Every competitor in the Eisteddfod has to send his name and address, in a sealed envelope, with his manuscript. When the adjudicators decide upon the winner, the sealed envelope is opened. In small eisteddfodau, this is usually done on the day of the eisteddfod. But at the National, it has to be done beforehand, because the winning compositions are published in a book, and the book is on sale to the public immediately after the Chairing Ceremony."

"Good !" said the Chief. "That means you can get his name and address from the Secretary ?"

"I won't trouble him," replied Hopkyn. "The names and addresses of all the winners are published in the book. I'll buy a copy so that I can read his poem. I want to know more about the poet than his name and address."

The Chief had another brainwave.

"Tell me, Hopkyn, about how many people compete for the Chair ?"

"The number varies. Usually, it's between twenty and thirty."

"These bards, they're a queer lot. Dressing up in those robes and things. Emotional. Hysterical. Jealous of one another. If one of them had sweated on getting the Chair, and another got it, he might feel so vicious that . . . what are you grinning at ?"

"Sorry, Chief, I couldn't help it. The idea of a disappointed bard waiting with a gun to kill the prizewinner is too good to be true. I grant you, Chief," he hastened to add, "that they're often a quarrelsome lot. After every National, there's always a lot of bickering about the prize compositions, especially the poems. Tempers get frayed, and a lot of abuse gets thrown about. But Welsh literary criticism—so far, at least—has stopped short of murder. A cynical critic may sometimes write that it would do Welsh poetry a world of good to get rid of some of the poets, but nobody as yet has had the courage of his convictions." Hopkyn went on talking because he could see that the Chief still felt nettled. "But what you've just said, Chief, does bring up the first question that we should ask ourselves about this murder. Was the Chair Bard shot because he happened to be the Chair Bard, or because he was himself ? Who was murdered—the Bard or the man ?"

The Chief looked puzzled.

"The Bard or the man ? Damn it all, Hopkyn, there was only one fellow shot, whatever you call him."

"Let me put it in another way. Would a murder have been committed if somebody else had won the Chair ? Would the Chair Bard have been shot whoever he happened to be ?"

"You mean that there was somebody waiting with a gun ready to shoot anyone who won the Chair ?"

"It's a possibility that we have to bear in mind."

"It's a terrible suggestion, Hopkyn ! Only a maniac would do it !"

"There are homicidal maniacs, Chief, people who kill for the sake of killing. Shooting the Chair Bard, with thousands of people looking on, could appeal to a certain type of mental pervert."

"You really believe it could be a maniac ?"

"I'm only considering the possibilities at the moment. That's why I asked if it was the man or the Bard that was shot. All we know about the murdered man is that he won the Chair. Was he shot for that reason ? We don't know. We can't know the reason for the shooting until we discover the motive, and we can't discover the motive until we know more about him. The Eisteddfod book will give us his name and address . . ."

"We'll soon find out more about him once we know who he is."

"I'll leave that end to you, Chief. While you're getting the material facts of his life, I'll read the poem to see if I can find anything else about him. You find out what other people can tell you about him, and I'll see if he can tell me something about himself. We may get somewhere then."

8. Dual Personality

The Eisteddfod Volume, an annual publication, is a thick paper-covered book of over 300 closely-printed pages. It contains all the poems that have been awarded prizes at the Eisteddfod, and also some of the prize compositions in prose—the short story, the *belle lettres*, essays, etc. The longer prose pieces, such as the novel and the play, are published in separate volumes.

The main portion of the book is taken up by the adjudications. The major competitions are judged by three adjudicators, each of whom submits a detailed criticism of the entries received.

The book is not on sale until Thursday afternoon, immediately after the Chairing Ceremony. The name of the winning bard is kept a close secret until it is announced from the stage by the Archdruid. This year, the name of the Chair Bard had not been announced, and there was a greater rush than ever for copies of the book. The first printing of five thousand copies was soon exhausted.

His name was David Beynon. His address was The Wayside Inn, Llanhelyg. Hopkyn looked up the place on a road-map. It was a little village in Flintshire, just within the Welsh border.

The title of the Chair Ode was "The Forest". It was a fairly long poem, just under three hundred lines. It was written in strict metre, which in Welsh is called *cynghanedd*. There is no English word for it. *Cynghanedd* is uniquely and peculiarly Welsh, and is never used seriously in English poetry even by Welsh poets writing in English. Not seriously. There have been occasional instances of writing English *cynghanedd* as a joke, for the fun of it. Twm o'r Nant, for example, an eighteenth century poet, on being refused lodgings at a Chester inn, protested to the janitor in a couplet of *cynghanedd*—

> *No bed, man, an' I bid money ?*
> *May your town go down the Dee !*

The two lines of this couplet illustrate two different types of *cynghanedd*. In the first type, the line is divided into two parts, and the consonants in the first part must be repeated in the same sequence in the second part—

> *No bed man | an' I bid money*
> *N   B D M N | N   B D M N*

The vowels in the two parts must be different, and the stressed accent in both parts must fall between M and N.

The second line is divided into three parts, not two ; the end syllable of the first part must rhyme with the end syllable of the second part ; and the stressed consonant preceding the second rhyme must be repeated in the third part—

> *May your town | go down | the Dee*
> *town   down   D . . .*

In all, there are four types of *cynghanedd*, each with its own rigid regulations. Like most literate Welshmen, Hopkyn could recognise and appreciate *cynghanedd* when he read or heard it, but he had only an elementary knowledge of the rules governing it. He knew that these rules were strict, complicated, full of pitfalls for the inexperienced.

What had the three adjudicators written of David Beynon's prize poem ? Hopkyn decided to see what they had to say about it before reading the ode himself.

"A great poem . . . shows a mastery of *cynghanedd* . . . a thrilling story vividly told . . . an allegory of our times written by a second Bunyan."

Praise laid on a bit too thick, thought Hopkyn. What about the second adjudicator ?

"A difficult poem to understand at the first reading . . . the story of the fighting is told simply and starkly, but vividly . . . the allegorical significance demands more thought from the reader."

The third adjudicator enlarged upon this :

"The poem," he wrote, "tells the story of a small group of soldiers fighting for their lives in the Malayan jungle. Night encompasses them ; insects, vermin, and snakes attack them ; the smell of decay sickens them ; the undergrowth tears at their limbs ; the brigands kill them off, one by one, until only twelve are left. These twelve fight on, blazing a path for other troops to follow. They are the pioneers, fighting not only to save their own lives, but to save the jungle for civilisation, so that the generations of the future can get rubber from its sap, timber from its trees, light and power from the dark rivers in its depths. The story, told in vivid language much helped by the *cynghanedd*, grips at the first reading ; but the strength of the poem goes deeper than the story, and lies in its allegorical significance. The jungle is the world we live in ; the darkness is the suspicion bred of ignorance ; the insects, vermin and snakes are the human vices which weaken the faith of those fighting for a better world ; the undergrowth is the disputes and conflicts, political and industrial, which impede progress. But there is in this great poem none of the despair and despondency so rife among our younger poets today. Here is a poet who faces the fifties with a challenge. Reading this poem should help us all to meet that challenge."

Hopkyn turned to the poem, and began to read. The language was not quite as simple as the adjudicators had led him to expect. There were words and phrases which he had to read more than once to assimilate. It was certainly a poem that needed more than one reading.

The story of the fighting in the forest was told in the first person by the sergeant left in charge of the survivors when the lieutenant leading the group was shot in the first ambush. Told in short stark sentences, the story gripped from the first word. It was during the cold, long, lonely watches of the night, when he meditated upon the world outside, that the sergeant unobtrusively slipped into allegory. So cleverly was it done that Hopkyn was glad that he had read the adjudicators' remarks before tackling the poem himself. There was no over-stressing of the allegory, no loud pedal in its application. It was so allusive as to be elusive. It was not until he had read the final epilogue—which described the jungle cleared of its undergrowth, its timber building houses for the homeless, its waters giving light and power to lonely villages—that the accumulative power of the allegory struck him with full force. Like *Pilgrim's Progress*, mused Hopkyn, it may all be a dream ; but, again like Bunyan, it was a poet's dream.

The fighting, however, was not a dream. Whoever wrote this poem had had first-hand experience of jungle warfare. It was not a journalistic mosaic made up of bits of other people's stories. The man who wrote this had been through it himself. He might have dreamt the allegory : but he didn't dream the fighting. David Beynon may have looked like a gigolo on that couch, but he had fought like a man in the jungle. He—

"Hello, Hopkyn ! Finished it ?"

The Chief had come in, and Hopkyn put the book down.

"Yes," he said. "Did you get through to Llanhelyg ?"

"There was a queue of reporters waiting for the hotel

56

telephone," grumbled the Chief. "I slipped across the road to the Police Station, and put in a priority police call." He chuckled loudly. "They were still cursing when I came in just now."

"Any news of Beynon ?"

"Not much. I rang up Jones, the village constable at Llanhelyg, but he was out. His wife answered the phone, and Jones will ring me back as soon as he comes home."

"Did she know David Beynon ?"

"She'd seen him around a few times, she said. Didn't know him well. He hadn't been there long."

"You told her he was dead ?"

"Yes. Thought I'd better. Didn't want his wife, if he were married, to hear the news all of a sudden on the radio. I asked Mrs. Jones to break it to her as gently as she could."

"That was considerate of you, Chief."

"No need for it. Beynon wasn't married. No family either. Been there only a few months, she said."

"He was only staying at The Wayside Inn ?"

"No, no, he lived there. I asked her if he was the landlord, and she said he was. Bought the place last January. Got a manageress there. A Miss Harris."

"What's the place like ?"

"Usual kind of roadhouse, from what she told me. Caters for the bright young things who frequent such places. Young fools in sports-cars. Cocktail parties. Saturday night dances. Young girls who try to look older, and old ones who try to look young. You know the type."

Hopkyn sat up.

"What's wrong, Hopkyn ? You look a bit startled."

"I am. You're quite sure Mrs. Jones got the right address ? She didn't mix it with another Llanhelyg pub ?"

"Couldn't have. There's only one pub there. The Plough. I stayed there for a week's fishing a couple of years ago."

"But isn't The Wayside Inn at Llanhelyg ?"

"It's three miles out, said Mrs. Jones. I told you it was a roadhouse, didn't I ?"

"That is what startled me. Sit down, Chief, and I'll tell you why. I've just been reading the Chair Ode, and I'd like you to hear some of it . . ."

"Don't waste your breath, lad. Can't stand poetry. Except for a limerick or two . . ."

"All right, Chief," smiled Hopkyn, "I'll let you off. But this David Beynon puzzles me, and the more I learn about him, the more puzzled I get. When I first saw him lying on the couch in the Secretary's room at the Eisteddfod pavilion, the first thought that struck me was that he looked more like a gigolo than a poet."

"That's exactly what I thought myself, Hopkyn."

"I had to remind myself that the history of literature is full of poets who looked like gigolos. Aristophanes, thousands of years ago, made fun of them. They have been the butt of every satirist through the ages. Racine, Sheridan, Shaw—they've all made fun of the type. But the fact remains that many of these gigolo poets have written some very readable verse, even if it isn't great poetry. Clever, slick, sophisticated—"

"Like that Oscar Wilde fellow, eh ?"

"And lots of others, Chief, before and after him. Too superficial to be sincere, too sensuous to be sensitive, but good stuff of its kind—hothouse verse, as somebody described it. We haven't had much of it in Welsh, possibly because it's a product of the city, not of the open air. When I first saw David Beynon, I took it for granted that he had written that kind of poetry, and that the newness of the thing in Welsh had won him the Chair. But when I read the ode, I had to change my mind. No gigolo could have written this poem . . ."

"Why not ?"

"Simply because that kind of poet couldn't possibly write this kind of poetry. The philosophic content of the work—"

"Eh ?"

"All right, Chief," chuckled Hopkyn, "I'll spare you

the metaphysics. But here's something you'll appreciate. The poem tells the story of a group of soldiers fighting for their lives in the jungles of Malaya—"

"Good Lord ! Is that what it's about ?"

"You and I, Chief, have been trained to weigh up evidence, to distinguish between a true story and a false one—"

"Just a minute, Hopkyn ! I've been led up the garden path more than once by a well-told tale."

"So have I, and it has made me all the more suspicious of well-told tales. You and I have suspicious minds—"

"Got to, in our job."

"But the story in this poem rings true, Chief. I'm convinced, absolutely convinced, that the man who wrote it described his own experience. It's not a made-up story."

"You sound pretty sure about it, Hopkyn."

"I'm dead sure. Before I came to you in North Africa, I had spent the best part of a year in Burma—"

"Yes, I remember that."

"I know what jungle warfare is. And so does the author of this poem. He's fought there. It made me change my mind about David Beynon. I kicked myself for letting myself be deceived by appearances. The pencilled moustache, the sleek hair, the manicured nails, those external details had made me build up a mental image of David Beynon that was wrong and slanderous. The real David Beynon, the man who wrote this poem, was a very different person. And then—just as I had switched from one mental image to another—you come in and tell me that David Beynon was the landlord of a cheap and vulgar roadhouse—"

"I don't know about cheap and vulgar, Hopkyn. There's nothing wrong in keeping a roadhouse if it's properly conducted."

"Nothing legally wrong, perhaps, but psychologically there's something very wrong indeed in this instance. It wouldn't be at all difficult to visualise the author of this poem in a quiet country pub, drawing pints of beer in the bar, or sweeping the yard with a broom, or even shovelling dung in a pigsty. But I can't see him mixing with the roadhouse type, drinking pink gins and telling smutty stories—no, no, Chief! He doesn't belong to that crowd."

"Let's get this straight, Hopkyn. When you first saw Beynon, you thought he was the gigolo type, smooth, slick, sophisticated ?"

Hopkyn nodded.

"And then, when you read his poem, you changed your mind. He might look like a gigolo, but he was a good poet and a damn good chap ?"

Hopkyn nodded again.

"And now, having heard that he kept a roadhouse, you feel puzzled about him ?"

"So puzzled that I must find out more about him. How far is it to Llanhelyg by road ?"

"Let's see. Forty, twenty, and another sixteen—about seventy-six miles."

"If I started off straight after breakfast tomorrow morning, I could be at The Wayside Inn before lunch. May I borrow your car, Chief ?"

"I'll get you a faster car than the little Austin. Ten o'clock tomorrow morning ?"

"Yes."

"Right. Best thing we can do now is to go to the Police Station and wait for Jones to ring up. He might be able to help you. Local knowledge."

The Police Station was just across the road. It was an ordinary double-fronted dwelling-house. The only visible difference between it and the other houses in the same terrace was the notice POLICE STATION above the front door, and an annexe at the back fitted up as a cell.

Sergeant Roberts was coming out of the house when the Chief Constable and Hopkyn arrived at the door.

"Just coming to fetch you, sir," explained the Sergeant. "Jones of Llanhelyg is on the phone."

"Good. Lead the way, Sergeant."

He led them to a room that took Hopkyn back to the

days of his own childhood. It looked exactly like the front parlour of his mother's old home. The horsehair sofa, the padded armchairs, the antimacassars, the ornaments, the faded photographs in their plush frames— everything was primly Victorian. Obviously, deduced Hopkyn, the Sergeant is a bachelor, with his mother or a widowed aunt keeping house for him. The only modern piece of furniture in the room was an office desk pushed out of the way into the far corner.

The Chief followed Roberts to the desk, picked up the telephone, and spoke.

"Chief Constable speaking . . . That's all right, Jones, no need to apologise . . . Gave you a bit of a shock, I suppose ? . . . Eh ? What's that you said ? . . . Good Lord ! Here, hold on. Detective Inspector Hopkyn, from Scotland Yard, wants a word with you. He's in charge of the case."

The Chief put down the receiver, and turned to Hopkyn with an amused glint in his eyes.

"Bit of a character, this Jones," he remarked. "Said that the news about Beynon winning the Chair gave him a bigger shock than the news of his death. Then he started jabbering about *cynghanedd* and things. You talk to him, Hopkyn."

Hopkyn picked up the receiver with a chuckle.

"This is Inspector Hopkyn, Jones. Tell me, are you an authority on *cynghanedd* ?"

The reply came in a voice redolent of the countryside— deep, slow, rich.

"I wouldn't sort of call meself an authority like . . ."

"But you do know the rules ?"

"Oh yes, I know the rules all right. But it's easy to get mixed up with the *Gwawdodyn Byr Degsillafog* and the *Llosgyrnog* and one or two others. And then there's . . ."

Jones was certainly a devotee of *cynghanedd*, and was quite prepared to discuss its multitudinous rules for hours on end. Hopkyn waited until Jones had to pause for breath, and then cut in.

"I intend coming to see you tomorrow, Jones, and I'd

like to have your opinion of Beynon's poem. I'll bring you a copy of the Eisteddfod volume—"

"I always order a copy in advance, sir, and I'll get it by first post tomorrow."

"Good. That will give you time to read it before I arrive. Can you meet me at The Wayside Inn at half-past twelve ?"

"Yessir."

"I suppose we could have lunch there ?"

"I don't know about that, sir. There's not much doing there in the daytime. But I'm sure Miss Harris could put on some ham an' eggs, if that would do. Are you teetotal, sir ?"

"Definitely not, Jones. Why ?"

"That's fine." There was a tremendous relief in the constable's voice. "There's some very good beer there."

"Ring Miss Harris tomorrow morning, Jones, and ask her to lay on ham, eggs, pickles and beer for both of us. Right ?"

"Thank you very much, sir."

"Just one question before I ring off. You told the Chief Constable just now that the news about Beynon winning the Chair gave you a bigger shock than the news of his death. Why ?"

"Well, sir, you know how it is, there's somebody or other falling down dead somewhere every day, isn't there ? It happens so often that it doesn't surprise us very much unless it takes place on our own doorstep, as it were. But when the Chair of the National Eisteddfod is won by a bard who hasn't written any *cynghanedd* before, it's—well, it's a bloody miracle. Beg your pardon, sir, for swearing out loud on the telephone, but all the same, it is damn funny, isn't it ? Lots of people were more than a bit surprised when Rowland Hughes won the Chair at the Machynlleth National in 1937, the first time he won it. Very few people knew, you see, that he could write *cynghanedd*, seeing that he hadn't published any, or very very little. We knew he was a poet all right, but all his work had been in the free metres, not the strict. This

David Beynon, however, was a different kettle of fish—"

"He hadn't written any poetry at all, free or strict ?"

"He hadn't published any, not over his own name."

"And he knew nothing about *cynghanedd* ?"

"Don't talk soft, man—sorry, sir, I forgot I was talking to an Inspector."

"That's all right, Jones. Carry on. The fact that he won the Chair proves that he could write in *cynghanedd*. Is that what you mean ?"

"To tell the gospel truth, sir, I don't know what the hell I mean. He's got me fair puzzled."

"You're not the only one, Jones. But we'll thrash it out together over a pint of beer at The Wayside Inn tomorrow. Half-past twelve, Jones."

"I'll be there waiting for you, sir."

"Good. Good-bye, Jones."

"Good-bye, sir."

9. Poet's Pub

Hopkyn stopped the car at the top of the hill, and looked at the clock on the dashboard. The Chief's official car was a Rover, there had been surprisingly little traffic on the way, and Hopkyn had made good time. It was now a few minutes after noon.

The Wayside Inn stood at the bottom of the hill, a hundred yards away. Hopkyn looked down at it, and frowned. He hadn't liked the place when he first saw it, and the more he looked at it the less he liked it.

It had been, once upon a time, a coaching inn. There was a big courtyard in front of the building, and a road led past the gable end of the house to another yard at the back, where the stables had been. These had been converted into lock-up garages : the cobbled surface of the two yards, and the road connecting them, was now a smooth stretch of concrete.

I don't mind that so much, mused Hopkyn. A landlord

must live, and when horses became horse-power concrete had to replace cobbles. It's what has been done to the house itself that annoys me. They have used paint and plaster, much too lavishly, to make a public show of its old age. Old age should be quiet, tranquil, serene. This place flaunts its age, makes a vulgar and gaudy parade of it. It's like some of those old ladies whom Wilfred Pickles used to bring to the microphone. They sang a raucous song in a cracked voice, and he told us over and over again how wonderful they were for their age. Probably made them a damn nuisance at home for the rest of their lives.

A poet's pub ? God forbid !

His eyes strayed past the inn, along the road to Llanhelyg, a little village skirting the foothills three miles away.

Constable Jones will have already started on his way, said Hopkyn to himself. If he's walking, I might as well go to meet him. It's a hot day for walking.

The hedge cast a narrow shadow, like a streak of black pavement, along the side of the road. A quarter of a mile beyond the inn, a mountain ash in full leaf threw a larger shadow half across the road. Hopkyn's eyes, half-closed against the whiteness of the road, focussed on the foot of this tree. There was somebody sitting there.

Hopkyn smiled. Constable Jones was also early, and was now sitting in the shade of the tree waiting for half-past twelve. Hopkyn released the brake, coasted down the hill, passed the inn, and the car came quietly to rest opposite the tree.

So silently had it arrived that it was only the slight squeak of the brakes which awoke Jones from his reverie. His helmet had been pushed back on the crown of his head ; below it, a round red face with two tufts of redder hair, a large freckled forehead glistening with sweat, and a bushy walrus moustache, looked rather askance at Hopkyn.

"Constable Jones ?" asked Hopkyn.

Jones gulped, pushed his pipe, still alight, into one

pocket, and the Eisteddfod book into another, and clambered clumsily to his feet.

"Yessir," he said, and walked into the road, buttoning up his tunic as he went.

"Come into the car," said Hopkyn, "I want a talk with you before we go into the inn."

Jones walked round the car, clambered in beside Hopkyn, placed his helmet on his knees, and prepared himself for a reprimand which never came.

"First things first, Jones. Before discussing the poem, I want you to tell me all you know about Beynon."

"Well, sir, it's not very much I know about him, I'm sorry to say. I went to see Miss Harris last night, sir, and I told her about his death—"

"How did she take it?"

"Bit shocked, of course, but she's not the sort to jump into sterricks."

"Into what?"

"Sterricks. Getting excited and throwing a fit and all that. You know."

"Hysterics. What did she say?"

"Worrying a little she was about keeping the place open. Thought she should perhaps close the pub, in respect to the dead, like. But a carload of young people came in just then, and ordered a round of drinks, and I suppose she thought it less trouble to serve them than to explain why she couldn't. Anyway, they got their drinks."

"And you your pint, Jones, eh?"

"Well, sir, I . . . er . . ."

Hopkyn laughed.

"Forget I'm an Inspector, Jones. Relax. I'm not the type to jump down a Constable's throat if I find him smoking on duty in a quiet country lane, or if he has his tunic unbuttoned on a hot afternoon. Or even if he sits on the roadside reading poetry."

Jones looked at him through the corner of his eye, and a slow smile spread over his face.

"Thankee, sir. We village policemen are a bit different from the smart fellows in town—"

65

Hopkyn nodded.

"I was born and bred in a small Welsh village, Jones. I know all about it. But what about Beynon ? Did Beynon fit into village life ?"

Jones shook his head.

"No, he didn't mix with us villagers. Very seldom it was he came into the village . . ."

"But surely some of the villagers went to his pub ?"

"Some of the younger fellows did, those who liked dolling up to meet the girls. But there wasn't a proper bar there, you see, nowhere to sit in comfort for a pint of beer. The place was too posh, full of little tables with glass tops, and those coloured wicker chairs which get out of shape when somebody as big as me squeezes into them. It was more like a caffy than a pub."

"Was it always like that ?"

"Good heavens, no ! It was a very nice old pub before Beynon bought it. I used to call there quite a lot—" He stopped abruptly, and added rather lamely, "Well, not too often, you know, just when I happened to be passing."

"And you happened to be passing fairly often, eh ?" grinned Hopkyn. "When did Beynon take over ?"

"On the first of January."

"This year ?"

"That's right. Eight months ago. Mrs. Thomas, who owned the place before him, took the family furniture away with her, and Beynon painted the place top to bottom, and bought a lot of new stuff to furnish it. Spent money like water, said Miss Harris, the manageress who took over when Miss Powell left. If you ask me, sir, I don't think Miss Harris cares very much for it. I remember telling her, soon after she came here, how nice the place looked after it had been made modern like. Of course, it wasn't my real opinion, I just said it to please her, being polite, you see. And she looked at me with a sort of twisted grin on her face, as if she pitied me, an' then she said that the sort of customers who come here seemed to like it."

66

"Well, I suppose an old lady of her age would prefer a quieter . . ."

"Miss Harris an old lady ? No, no ! She's quite young, just left college."

Hopkyn sat up.

"Just left college ?" he repeated. "Let's get this straight, Jones. How old is Miss Harris ?"

"I should say about twenty four or twenty five."

"About the same age as Beynon ?"

"There or thereabouts.'

"And Beynon put her in charge as soon as he bought the place ? "

"Oh no. Miss Harris has only been here a few weeks. She took on a job as assistant cook here for the summer holidays, but when old Sarah Powell—the housekeeper that was here with Mrs. Thomas—when old Sarah Powell quarrelled with the new master—"

"What did they quarrel about ?"

"Sarah felt like a fish out of the water when the place was done up new. And she didn't hold with the dancing, and the young people drinking too much. So she gave Beynon a month's notice, and left."

"But surely, wasn't Miss Harris far too inexperienced to look after a hotel ?"

"You haven't met Miss Harris, have you, sir ?"

"Not yet."

"She's young, very young, but she's all there. I like her very much."

"And so, apparently, did Beynon. Was his liking for her restricted to business relations, Jones ?"

"You mean did they live tally ?"

"Live what ?'

"Live tally." Jones smiled. "Good word, isn't it ? Comes from the Italian. In the old days, all gipsies were called Italians, and as they never married respectable in church or chapel, it was called to live tally."

"I see. Did Beynon and Miss Harris live tally ?"

"I don't think so. She doesn't strike me as that sort of girl."

"Did Beynon go with any other woman, or women ? Any talk about him in the village ?"

"He was a ladies' man right enough, and very popular with young women. Much the same crowd came to the inn every Saturday night, they tell me, and Beynon was the life and soul of the party. But I haven't heard of him having any special woman friend like."

"Had he any other interest, apart from the hotel ? You said on the phone that you were more than a little surprised that he had won the Chair. You must have known him fairly well to say that ?"

"No, I didn't know him at all well, sir. In fact, I had only one long talk with him—"

"But look here, Jones ! You can't possibly tell if a man is a good poet or not after only one talk with him."

"It was like this, sir. He came to see me some time in February, and said he'd like to have a Welsh party in the inn on March the first, St. David's Day. A *Noson Lawen* we call it, a free-for-all with singing and folk-dancing and harp music and poetic competitions and so on. He knew I was the captain of the local *Ymryson y Beirdd* team—"

"What team is that ?"

"Don't you ever listen to the wireless, sir ?"

"Not very often, Jones. And I can't get the Welsh programmes where I live."

"Oh. That's a pity, that is. *Ymryson y Beirdd* is a bardic competition. The poets of one place issue a challenge to the poets of some other place—village against village, or town against town—and there's a Chaired Bard of the National Eisteddfod—Meuryn his name is—who acts as referee, and he gives the two teams a line of poetry in *cynghanedd* for them to add another line to it to make a couplet of *cywydd*—but perhaps you don't know what a *cywydd* is, sir ?"

"Carry on, Jones. A *cywydd* is a piece of poetry written in couplets of *cynghanedd*. I know that much."

"Every member of a team has to know the rules pretty well to make a couplet in the little time he gets to make one, but I had a jolly good team last winter, and we beat

68

all the others. Dafydd William of Hendy is leaving Llanhelyg this September, and I'm looking for somebody to take his place in the team. Well, sir, at this *Noson Lawen* we had, Beynon was the Chairman, and he recited such a lot of Welsh poetry, in *cynghanedd* too, that I thought he might make a good member for my team. So I wrote him an *englyn* to praise him as Chairman, and gave it to him. You know what an *englyn* is, sir ?"

"Yes. A stanza of thirty syllables in four lines."

"And in *cynghanedd*, of course. He read the *englyn*, and thanked me very much for it. He'd get it framed, he said, and hang it up in the hall where everybody could see it."

"Why are you grinning, Jones ?"

"He praised it too much, sir. There were three mistakes of *cynghanedd* in that englyn. I had put them in to test him, see ? Anybody who knew anything about *cynghanedd* would have seen the first mistake. It hit you in the eye, so to speak. The second one was not so obvious, but a good man at *cynghanedd* would spot it quick enough. The third was a bit tricky. It looked all right, but it wouldn't have deceived a bard like Meuryn, not by a long chalk."

"It did deceive Beynon ?"

"Beynon didn't find any of the three mistakes."

"You can't be sure of that, Jones. He might have seen them, but as a matter of courtesy refrained from drawing your attention to them."

"You mean he didn't want to hurt my feelings like ? Oh no, I thought of that. You see, when he spoke of framing the *englyn* and hanging it up in the hall, I got the wind up. People who knew what's what would read it there, see the mistakes, and my name under it. I'd be a bloody laughing-stock, wouldn't I ? So I told him that I wasn't quite sure about the *cynghanedd* in one line. I actually pointed to the first mistake, and asked him if I had better change the word. If he knew anything at all of *cynghanedd*, he'd have known then that I was putting his knowledge to the test—"

Hopkyn chuckled.

"Jones," he said, "you're the first detective-poet I've

69

ever met. But tell me this. If Beynon could not write *cynghanedd*, how the hell did he win the Chair ?"

"That's what gave me the shock, sir."

"Did he pay someone for writing the ode ?"

Jones looked at him, aghast.

"Don't be daft, man. Oh ! Sorry, sir, I—"

"Why is the idea so daft ?"

"Good heavens, man ! The ambition of every poet in Wales is to win the Chair at the National ! A man would sell his soul to win it !"

"That's all very well, Jones, but you have just assured me that Beynon couldn't have written the poem himself. Now you tell me that he couldn't have hired any other poet to write it for him. There's only one other possibility. Did he steal the poem from somebody ?"

"How could he, sir ?"

"There must be heaps of old manuscripts lying around, especially in old houses. Take The Wayside Inn for example. He may have come across an old poem—"

Hopkyn paused suddenly.

"All right, Jones, tell me I'm talking through my hat. Am I ?"

"Sorry, sir, I'm afraid you are, rather. The poem is about jungle fighting in Malaya—"

"Oh damn ! Of course it is. It couldn't have been an old manuscript. It must be the work of a modern poet. But who ?"

Hopkyn puffed at his pipe for a minute, or two, and then slowly turned to face Jones.

"Jones, the news of Beynon's death didn't give you much of a shock, you said. Would you feel a bigger shock if I told you that his death was not a natural one ?"

Jones nodded, quietly and calmly.

"I suspected there was something unnatural about it. They wouldn't send a famous detective from Scotland Yard to investigate a natural death."

"He was shot through the heart."

"Ah !"

They looked at each other.

"The same thought has struck you too, Jones. Hasn't it ?"

"It's too obvious, if you ask me."

"But it gives a motive for the crime."

"Hmmm." Jones shook his head. "If Beynon won the Chair with a stolen poem, why did the fellow who wrote the poem have to shoot him ? All he had to do was to get up on his feet and accuse Beynon of stealing his work. It wouldn't take five minutes to prove that Beynon couldn't have written it himself. Shooting Beynon wouldn't get him the Chair, would it ? The gallows, more likely."

"But if, for the sake of argument, we assume that Beynon did win the Chair with somebody else's poem, then we are faced with two alternatives, one of which must be true. Beynon got the poem with the owner's consent, or without it. You've already told me that Beynon could recite a lot of poetry. Even if he couldn't write any himself, he might have been a good critic of poetry. Let's suppose somebody shows him this poem. Beynon likes it, and asks if he may borrow the poem for a day or two to study it in more detail. The author lets him have it, and on the way home is run over by a car, or has a heart attack, or dies suddenly in some other way. He has told Beynon that nobody knows anything about the poem, so Beynon sends it to the Eisteddfod in his own name."

"And on the day he is chaired," said Jones, solemnly, "the dead author rises from the grave and shoots him. Is that what you mean, sir ?"

Hopkyn grinned.

"Jones," he said, with equal solemnity, "at this moment, it's you I'd like to shoot. All right, here's another theory. See what you can do to this one. Beynon likes the poem, but the author doesn't think so much of it. Righto, says Beynon, I'll give you a hundred pounds for it. It's a gamble, he says, but I think the gamble is worth it. A hundred pounds in hand is worth a Chair in the bush. You're shaking your head, Jones. What's wrong with it—with the theory, I mean, not with your head ?"

"Two objections, sir. If it was just a business deal, why the shooting ?"

"And the other objection ?"

"I've read the poem three times this morning. Whoever wrote it must have known he'd written one of the best odes of this century. He couldn't help knowing it. He'd never have sold it. And more than that, sir, this fellow was not only a good poet. He was—and I hope you won't laugh when I say this—he was a good man. You can feel when you're reading the poem that the man who wrote it was sincere and straight and honest. He's put his soul into it. And a man like him wouldn't sell his soul."

"You're right, Jones. I too felt something of the sort when I read the poem. He wrote from his heart. I could feel the man behind the poem, a man I could like and respect and admire. That's why I couldn't believe that such a man would keep a pub like The Wayside Inn. What you've told me about Beynon has confirmed my suspicions, Jones. Whoever wrote the Chair Ode, it wasn't David Beynon."

"But who was it, sir ?"

"That's what we'll have to find out. It may be the bigger mystery of the two. If we can solve the puzzle of the authorship, we may solve the murder also. All right, Jones, we'll go and have a chat with Miss Harris. Come on."

10. Miss Harris

The front lounge of The Wayside Inn shone with new paint and new furniture. Beynon, who had tried to make the outside of the inn look as old as possible, had exerted himself equally hard to make the inside look new. He had succeeded. Its newness bawled and jarred.

Jones stepped up to the small shining bar-counter in the far corner of the room, and rang the chromium-plated bell placed on its stainless-steel surface. A girlish

voice from the room beyond shouted "Coming !", and a
few moments afterwards Miss Harris appeared behind the
counter.

She was young, quietly dressed, and at first sight not at
all pretty. Her forehead was a shade too broad for her
face, her eyes were a little too far apart, and her mouth
was slightly too large for her nose. Not pretty, said
Hopkyn to himself, but very charming. And, if I'm not
mistaken, with a very shrewd head on her young shoulders.
I like her eyes—and then he realised why he liked them.
There was a family in his native village who had the same
eyes : slate blue, observant, humorously critical. She
looked out of place in this garish, artificial environment.
Neither in her dress nor in her make-up did Miss Harris
pay homage to the newness around her.

"Hello, Jones !" she said. "You look terribly hot and
bothered. Inspector Hopkyn, I presume ?"

Hopkyn smiled and nodded, and walked up to the bar.

"I won't keep you long, Miss Harris. Just a few
questions—"

"That's all right, Inspector. We've nobody staying
here, the maid's gone out for a walk, and the barman is
listening to a cricket commentary on the wireless. I'm
very glad to have somebody to talk to. But not in this
room." She paused, looked round the room with a slight
grimace, caught Hopkyn's eye, and smiled at him. "I've
got quite a cosy little room of my own behind the bar,
if you and Constable Jones would like to bring your beer
there with you."

It was, thought Hopkyn, a very nice way of asking them
to have a drink. In the mirror behind the bar, he caught a
reflection of Jones's face, looking at him very anxiously.
There was no need to enquire what was troubling the
Constable's mind. It wasn't the murder, nor the puzzle
of the authorship of the Chair Ode. Jones was wondering
whether Hopkyn was one of those Inspectors who refuse
to drink when on duty.

Hopkyn was not.

"There's nothing I should like better than a long drink," he replied. "And I'm sure Jones here feels the same."

Jones nodded vigorously.

"Thank you very much indeed, Miss Harris," said he. "And excellent beer it is, too."

Two firkins of beer stood on a stand behind the counter, each shrouded in a white cover embroidered with a jazzy design in many colours. Hopkyn looked at them wryly. The beer, however, showed no sign of contamination. The little chromium pump attached to the barrel emitted a frothy jet which spoke well of the beer's condition.

Miss Harris put the filled tankard on the counter.

"That's for the Inspector, Jones. It's bitter. You drink mild, don't you ?"

"Yes, please, miss."

Hopkyn smiled. Jones, who had told him he was not a frequent visitor to the inn, obviously came there often enough for Miss Harris to know which beer he preferred. But how the devil did she know that he, Hopkyn, drank bitter beer ?

"Your health, miss. And yours, sir."

Jones gulped half his pint in one mighty swallow, sucked in the fringe of his moustache, and smiled expansively.

"That's better," he said, and pulled out his pipe.

Miss Harris was looking at Hopkyn, with a slightly puzzled frown on her wide forehead.

"I hope I haven't made a mistake, Inspector. It is bitter you drink, isn't it ?"

"Yes," smiled Hopkyn. "But how did you know ?"

"My father happened to mention it one day."

"Your father ! Do I know him ?"

"You should. You went to school with him at Aberywen. You lived next door to him at the time."

"Will Harris ! Good gracious, are you Will's daughter ?"

"I am. You couldn't possibly remember me, of course."

"But I do. I remember the last time I saw you. It was on a Friday night when Will was trying to give you a bath.

74

Your mother had gone to bed with a headache, and I helped Will to bath you. We weren't quite sure how to take off your clothes—"

He broke short. Once again he had caught a reflection of Jones's face in the mirror behind the bar. It was one big question mark.

Hopkyn laughed.

"It's all right, Jones, don't look so shocked. Miss Harris was a very small baby at that time. I left Aberywen soon afterwards, but though I've been going there for an occasional holiday from time to time, I don't think we've met since then. Or have we ?"

"You used to come there when I was either at college or on holiday from home. But I did see you once, a couple of years ago. I came home the day you were leaving Aberywen, and I saw you passing in the car. Father told me who you were, and that's how I recognised you today. But come through to my room. I hate this lounge."

They followed her into a cosy, quiet room with large, comfortable, old-fashioned chairs. A small table, covered with writing paper, stood below the window.

"Here you are, Jones, this chair is big enough, even for you." She laughed suddenly. "I'll never forget the first time I met you. You came into the lounge and sat in one of those silly little wicker-chairs. When you got up to go out, the chair rose with you. We had to get the barman to prise it off."

Hopkyn was looking at the paper-strewn table by the window.

"Well, Jones," he said, "here's one mystery solved. When you told me that the manageress of this place was a young lady who had come here straight from college, I couldn't help wondering what her motive was." He turned to Miss Harris. "All he could tell me was that your name was Miss Harris. I didn't connect it with the Norma Harris who wrote *In Cap and Gown*, and who is presumably busy writing another novel."

"Did father send you a copy of my book ?"

75

"He did, and I enjoyed it very much. Did you come here to get material for another novel?"

Miss Harris shook her head.

"No. It was a far simpler reason, really. I wanted to be a journalist, and naturally went in for an arts degree. But it's terribly difficult to get a job in Fleet Street nowadays, and I hated the idea of starting on a provincial paper and having to write reports of inquests and council meetings. So I decided to stay at college for another couple of years to take a diploma in Domestic Science. I've always been fond of cooking, and a girl with a Domestic Science Diploma can easily get a job today. I saw an advertisement for an assistant cook at The Wayside Inn, Llanhelyg, and I applied for it. I didn't like the place when I saw it from the outside, and I detested it all the more when I went inside. But Mr. Beynon offered me very good wages, and was so insistent that I agreed to give it a month's trial."

"When was this?"

"Last June, when I left college. The cook-housekeeper, Sarah Powell, departed shortly afterwards, and Mr. Beynon offered me fifteen pounds a week to stay on as manageress. I didn't like to leave him in the lurch, so I stayed on."

"For the sake of the money and the experience?"

"Partly. You see, we don't take in residents, and the place is so remote that there's very little business here except on Wednesday and Saturday evenings. It's crowded out with young people on those two nights, and we have a buffet supper and a dance. But for the remainder of the week it is very quiet here—"

"And you have plenty of time for your writing?"

"Yes. That's what I liked best about the place—in fact, the only thing I liked about it. I have the place practically to myself for most of the week—"

"Wasn't Beynon here all the time?"

"No. He used to leave here early on Monday morning, and return for lunch on Wednesday. He'd leave again on Thursday morning, returning rather late on Friday."

"On business ?"

"I suppose so. I didn't ask, and he didn't tell me. As a matter of fact, I didn't very much care for him, and preferred to keep him at arm's length."

"Why ? Had he made any . . . er . . . ?"

Miss Harris laughed.

"Advances ? I'm no longer the little innocent you helped to bath, Inspector. There's no need for you to be shy. Beynon wasn't. The first thing I had to do when the cook left was to tell him, very bluntly, that I wasn't going to play that kind of ball with him. I explained to him that it wasn't the money, and still less his company, which induced me to stay. It was the quiet and the leisure to write."

"How did he take it ?"

"Very well. He realised that I was in earnest, and immediately switched the conversation to writing."

"Was he interested in books ?"

"Oh yes. And when he found out that I had already got my first book published, and that it had—well, not made any kind of a sensation, of course, but had been well received and was selling much better than I expected —he thought it would be quite a good advertisement for the place to have what he called a popular young novelist as manageress. The bright young things who come here made quite a fuss about it." Miss Harris smiled. "I became the show-piece of the place. You know the kind of thing—such a young girl in charge, my dear ! And a novelist too ! You should read her book, all about college ! Oh, yes, dear, she's been to college and all that. You *must* meet her !"

The mischievous glint in her eyes reminded Hopkyn of her father. Will had the same sense of humour.

"You've seen the papers this morning ?"

"Yes. And I'd like to thank you for sending Jones to break the news to me. I didn't care very much for my late boss, but it would have been a shock to read—"

"That's all right. Have you had any press reporters here today ?"

"No. Two came on the phone, and wanted to know what the place was like, and how the village had reacted to the news. They didn't sound very interested."

"Hm. I'm afraid there will be hordes of them here when the news breaks."

Miss Harris looked at him, very seriously, and then nodded quietly.

"I see. When Jones told me that there was an Inspector from Scotland Yard coming here to see me, I wondered what was behind it. The papers said that Mr. Beynon died of a heart attack. Did he ?"

"No. He was shot. Murdered."

"Shot ? But how could he have been shot, with all those people looking on ?"

Hopkyn told her what had happened.

"We've kept it dark," he added, "for two reasons. The Eisteddfod officials are afraid that the news of the shooting might keep people away from the Eisteddfod. The Chief Constable and I are afraid that it would bring crowds of people there for the wrong reason. Anyway, we think that there's a better chance of solving the murder if we can work at it in peace and quiet. What I am after now is a motive for the murder. If I can find out why Beynon was shot, I may be able to find out who it was that shot him. Do you know anything about Beynon which might help me to find a motive ?"

Miss Harris didn't reply immediately. She sat, quietly thinking. Hopkyn refilled his pipe, and left her to her thoughts. She knows what I want, he said to himself, there's no need to prompt her. Let her think it over, collect her thoughts, marshal her facts. She'll speak when she has something to tell me.

The silence grew. Jones fidgeted in his chair. His empty tankard made a small clatter on the table. Miss Harris turned her head to look at him, and sprang to her feet.

"I'm so sorry, Jones. Let me fetch you another drink."

"No, no, miss—"

"Of course you must. And you too, Inspector. I'm

afraid I won't be able to help you very much about Mr. Beynon, but I'll tell you all I know. You'll listen much better if you have a drink. You bring your own tankard, Jones, and I'll take the Inspector's."

Jones obeyed with alacrity.

Miss Harris sipped a sherry as she talked.

"I came here," she began, "on the third Monday in June, seven weeks ago. The cook left at the end of the month, and I have been manageress here for the past five weeks. When Mr. Beynon realised that I was not willing to fit in with his plans, and that I meant to keep myself to myself, I had no further trouble with him. He treated me very decently, and never interfered with my work. He had no previous experience of running a hotel, but Jim is an excellent barman, and he saw to it that the beer was all right. The maid is a local girl who sleeps in, and she and I, once we had the work properly organised, found no difficulty in looking after the house and preparing a buffet supper twice a week. The accountant, Mr. Hugheston, comes here every Saturday morning to help with the accounts. It is a small inn, the staff is small, and the overhead expenses are not very heavy. We sell a great deal of drink and food, especially spirits and cocktails, on Wednesday and Saturday nights, and the place shows a good profit. I don't care for the people who come here, but they seem to have plenty of money, and they don't mind spending it. Mr. Beynon was a very popular host, and they all seemed to hang around him a good deal. But he always kept himself, I noticed, on a fairly tight rein, and though he appeared to drink as much as anyone, I've never seen him drunk. More often than not, the whisky he had in his glass was really ginger-ale. He seemed a generous and lavish host, but I noticed that he knew very well when to stand a round of drinks on the house. It was always when most of the people had already been served at somebody else's expense. He made a pose of generosity, but took good care that it didn't cost him very much."

"That's right," said Jones. "Take the *Noson Lawen* we

79

had on St. David's Day. He stood us three drinks—one at the start, one half-way, and one to finish up with. Only three, mind. And they were half-pints !"

Jones still felt a sense of grievance.

"Did he buy this place outright ?" asked Hopkyn. "Or was he a tenant for one of the breweries ?"

"He owned the place."

"Any idea how much he gave for it ?"

"He was very secretive about money, but I believe it was in the region of fifteen thousand pounds."

"Quite a lot of money for a young man. How did he get it ?"

"He told me that he inherited his father's business when his mother died. His father, he said, had quite a large business at Caerefrog—The Book Emporium, one of the biggest and busiest shops in the town, selling books, newspapers, stationery, tobacco, sweets. His mother inherited the business when his father died, and when his mother died, he sold out and bought The Wayside Inn."

"I see. You said that he spent more than half the week away from here. Did you forward his letters ?"

"No."

"Did he tell you where he went ?"

"No. But he was always hail-fellow-well-met with most of the people who came here, and the impression I had was that he used to meet them during the week. See you on Tuesday, missed you last Thursday—that kind of thing."

"Where did these people come from ?"

"Lots of places. Liverpool, Wrexham, Chester, Shrewsbury. Some came from further afield—Coventry, Manchester, and so on."

"Were they always the same people ?"

"There were some who came regularly, week after week, but they often brought new faces with them."

"You mean the regulars touted for him ?"

Miss Harris hesitated.

"Well," she said slowly, "that's what it looked like. I had an idea once that Mr. Beynon was a commission agent, and that these were his runners. But though they talked a lot about dogs and horses, and spoke of bets they had won and lost, they were not the betting type one meets at races. At least, I don't think they were."

"Did you see any money passing between them and Beynon ?"

"No. But he could have given them money, or taken their money, without my seeing it. During the evening, he very often took them to his private room—"

"One at a time, or in groups ?"

"One at a time, usually. I've no idea what passed between them there."

"I'd very much like to have a look at his private room," said Hopkyn. "I haven't brought a search-warrant with me, and I've really no right to ask you—"

"Please don't stand on ceremony, Inspector," cut in Miss Harris. "I'll take you to the room, and leave you there. Jones said you'd like to lunch here. I can give you some soup—tinned, I'm afraid—a mixed grill, and some fruit salad. Coffee and biscuits too. And some cheese, of course. Will that do ?"

"Excellent. And with your permission, we'll have a look at the room while you get it ready."

"Good. This way, then."

Beynon's private room was at the end of the passage leading from the front door.

"Here you are," said Miss Harris as she unlocked the door for them. "I'll call you when lunch is ready."

11. Left Luggage

Beynon's private office was furnished in quieter taste than the lounge. The walls here also had been newly painted, but were in broken white, and the light brown paintwork harmonised with the tinge of umber used to break up the white.

Half-way up one wall had been shelved for books.

Hopkyn cast his eyes over the titles. They were a mixed lot. A complete set of Shaw occupied one shelf, Wilde and Swinburne shared another. Then came an assortment of Elizabethan dramatists, of whom Kyd and Greene and Lyly showed more wear than the others. A single-volume collection of Shakespeare's plays showed even more wear. There were a few Welsh books, mostly poetry. Gwynn Jones was well represented, and Williams Parry's volume of poems was well worn. Two shelves were filled with a good selection of the classics, in Dent's "Everyman" edition : most of these looked unopened, but Coleridge, Burns and Hazlitt had been dipped into more than once. The two bottom shelves contained an assorted mixture of American thrillers.

Between the books and the window stood a roll-top desk. It was closed, and when Hopkyn tried to open it, he found that it was also locked.

"An honest man's lock," commented Hopkyn. "Too simple a lock for the dishonest."

He took out of his pocket a small bunch of skeleton keys, and the lock clicked open at the first attempt. He pushed up the lid, and looked inside the desk.

"Very businesslike, Jones," he remarked. "I wish I could keep my desk half as tidy. Every pigeon-hole labelled—Accounts Due, Accounts Paid, Ministry of Food, Breweries, Letters Answered, and Pending. I may have to go through the whole lot later on, but not now." He paused. "Here, Jones, have a quick look through these Accounts Paid, while I look through the Accounts Due. You know what to look for, don't you ?"

Jones hesitated.

"I'm not quite sure, sir."

"That other business which took him four days from home every week."

"Ah ! Some funny business, eh ?"

"Might be. He wasn't very open about it, was he ? Anyway, see what the bills are for."

Hopkyn had gone through the unpaid bills long before Jones had finished the paid accounts. There was nothing "funny" about the unpaid ones. There were only six of them, and they were all for small amounts—the usual monthly accounts due to the baker, butcher, greengrocer, a bill for a sports-coat, and a statement from a tobacco firm.

The Ministry of Food pigeon-hole was full of forms and coupons, and the Breweries contained a further assortment of bills, paid and unpaid.

"Can't find anything funny about these, sir," reported Jones. "Most of the bills are from the painter and carpenter for repairs."

"All right, Jones, put 'em back. I'll skip through the letters. But they don't look very promising."

There were not many of them. Beynon had only kept those letters which he thought he might need for future reference. Somebody had sent him the name and address of a Liverpool tailor. There was a letter from the manager of a Manchester hotel assuring him that there would be a room at his disposal whenever possible. A garage in Coventry offered him a new Riley at list price.

Hopkyn skimmed through them all, and was putting them back into the pigeon-hole when he noticed that in taking them out he had left one letter behind. He opened it, read it, and turned to Jones.

"Do you know Caerefrog at all, Jones ?"

"I've been there a few times, sir. Why ?"

"This letter is from the manager of the Midland Bank at Caerefrog. It's rather an odd letter. Listen."

He read it out.

Tel. Caerefrog 631
December 15, 1950.

The Midland Bank,
Caerefrog.

D. Beynon Jones, Esq.,
The Book Emporium,
Caerefrog.

Dear Sir :
I beg to acknowledge receipt of your communication of the 13th inst. and note that for business reasons you propose

to adopt as surname your middle name of Beynon. I assume that you have already discussed with a solicitor the advisability of changing the name by deed poll. As far as your account in this Bank is concerned, I am of course prepared to honour cheques signed by you in the new name provided you will be good enough to submit, on the enclosed card, in triplicate, a copy of your new signature.

Yours faithfully,

IORWERTH PRYDDERCH,
Manager.

Hopkyn folded the letter and slipped it into his pocket.

"Beynon came here on the first of January. A fortnight before he came, he changed his name. Why ?"

"Perhaps he thought Jones wasn't swanky enough for a swell place like this."

Hopkyn chuckled.

"You may be right, Jones. It's possible that it was his only reason, and that I may be quite wrong in imagining something more sinister behind it. After all, a man doesn't write to tell his bank manager that he's changing his name if there's any fraudulent intent behind it. And yet, why all this secrecy about the weekly trips to Liverpool and Manchester and other places ? The more I get to know about Beynon, the less I seem to get to know him."

"I wish I could be more helpful, sir."

Jones looked so disconsolate that Hopkyn had to laugh.

"No, no, Jones, you and Miss Harris have helped all you could. It's like a jigsaw puzzle—the more pieces one collects, the bigger is the confusion until the pieces begin to sort themselves out. Oh well ! I'll have to keep on collecting more pieces before I can make anything of those I've got. Let's have a look in the drawers. Ah ! Locked. But all the drawers open if we unlock the top one. That shouldn't be difficult."

Nor was it : one of the skeleton keys fitted the lock, and the drawer was soon opened.

"Notepaper, postcards, envelopes. Nothing interesting here. Let's try the next drawer. A correspondence file—letters received, carbon copies of replies sent, etcetera. No time to wade through them now. What about the third drawer? Just a collection of rubbish—an old paint-box, a half-empty bottle of ink, a broken fountain-pen, a ball of string, lots of small cardboard boxes, two new typewriter ribbons—hello, what's this? A revolver. No, not a real one. A stage prop. And a dirty tin full of dirtier greasepaints. Amateur dramatics, probably. No good, Jones. Another mare's nest. We'll try the other side."

The top drawer on the right-hand side was also locked but the same key opened it.

"Good heavens! Full of pay envelopes. With the small staff working here, there are enough envelopes in this drawer to last a hundred years."

He paused suddenly.

"Ah! We'll take this drawer right out, Jones. Can you see what's wrong with it?"

Jones stared hard, and shook his head.

"Looks all right to me."

"Look at the front of the drawer, Jones. How deep is it?"

"About six inches, I should say."

"Yes. The envelopes inside it are stacked on end, and they're flush with the top of the drawer. See? I'll take one out. It's a square envelope. How big, Jones?"

"About four inches square—Ah! I see it now! There's a false bottom to the drawer."

"A very obvious one. We'll have a look what's inside it."

Inside the hidden partition were five bank passbooks. Each passbook was inscribed in a different name, but all the names had the same pair of initials—Donald Barry, Dave Bright, Desmond Brown, David Billing, and Derek Bowen.

Each passbook had been issued at a different town—Liverpool, Manchester, Coventry, Shrewsbury, Chester.

Each passbook was on a different bank—Lloyds, National Provincial, Barclays, Westminster, Martins.

They were all current accounts, and at weekly intervals substantial sums of money had been paid into each account.

Hopkyn laid the open books on the desk, and compared the last entry in each.

On July 24, Beynon had paid £70 into the Liverpool account, and £46 into the Chester account. On July 25, he had paid £76 into the Manchester account. On July 27, he had paid £54 into the Shrewsbury account, and on July 28 he had paid £62 into the Coventry account. This made a total of £308 for the week.

Hopkyn took out his diary, and looked up these dates. July 24 was a Monday, and Beynon on that date had visited Liverpool, probably breaking his journey at Chester. The following day, Tuesday, he was at Manchester. Miss Harris had said that he usually came home on Wednesday, and left again on Thursday. July 27 was a Thursday, and he had been to Shrewsbury, proceeding the following day, Friday, to Coventry.

The previous week, he had followed the same itinerary —Chester and Liverpool on Monday, Manchester on Tuesday, Shrewsbury on Thursday, Coventry on Friday. Some weeks had been very profitable, especially the second week in March, when he had paid in a total of £632. There were few weeks when he had failed to make £200 : the lowest was £144 in the last week in January. The average weekly total was around £300. Over £14,000 a year.

All five were current accounts. Why not deposit accounts, earning interest ? There could be only one reason, thought Hopkyn. Beynon knew that any account drawing over £25 p.a. interest would have to be disclosed to the Income Tax authorities. Beynon sacrificed the interest because he didn't want the accounts disclosed.

Was Miss Harris right ? wondered Hopkyn. Was Beynon a bookie ? If he was, why all the secrecy ? Black Market more likely : rationing was still in force. But in what ?

"Got something, sir ?" asked Jones.

"Yes, but I'm not sure what it means—yet. I'll take these passbooks with me. Put them in my bag, Jones. I'll replace the drawer and have a look inside the other two."

The second drawer was empty, but in the bottom drawer he found a paying-in book and a bank statement. These had been issued by a local bank, and were in the name of David Beynon. The bank statement showed that The Wayside Inn was making quite a good profit. The initial expenses had been heavy, but the wages bill was small, and at a rough computation the average weekly profit came to about £75. Not much, thought Hopkyn, and it would have taken a good many years at this rate for Beynon to get back the money he had spent on the place. But why carry on with the hotel when the other business, whatever it was, paid so much better? There was really no need for him to—

Suddenly, one of the jig-saw pieces slipped into place. If my guess is right, thought Hopkyn, The Wayside Inn is part and parcel of the other business. Not absolutely essential to it, perhaps, but very very useful.

He got up from the desk, pursed his lips at the small marble nude on the top of the desk, and was turning away when he noticed that the statuette was being used as a paperweight. There was an envelope underneath it. Hopkyn removed the nude and picked up the envelope.

The postmark was Liverpool, and the date August 5. Last Wednesday, he said to himself. But why keep an empty envelope? And why put a statuette on it to keep it safe?

But the envelope was not quite empty. Inside it, he found a ticket. The ticket had been issued at the Left Luggage Office, Lime Street Station, Liverpool. Like the envelope, it was dated August 5. The number it bore was 5643.

"No letter, sir?" asked Jones.

"Only a ticket," replied Hopkyn. "Posted last Wednesday. Probably delivered here on Thursday morning. Beynon was at the Eisteddfod on Thursday. When did he go there ? Did he leave here on Wednesday ? I should have asked Miss Harris."

"Must have got the letter before he left. Miss Harris wouldn't have opened it in his absence, would she ?"

"You're right, Jones. The letter must have come by the morning post on Thursday, Beynon opened it, may have been in a hurry to start off for the Eisteddfod, put it on the desk, and shoved the nude on it to keep it from blowing away."

"But why should anybody send him a Left Luggage ticket by post ?"

Hopkyn smiled.

"I can think of a dozen reasons, Jones. If I'm right— and I believe I am—there's one of them that fits. It may turn out to be the key piece to the jig-saw—the Left Luggage ticket, the pay envelopes, the deposit accounts and the travelling. I *must* be right, Jones ! Anyway, I can make sure by writing to the Liverpool C.I.D. today, send them the ticket, and ask them to ring me up to-morrow." He laughed aloud. "I'm on the trail at last ! Tell me, Jones, how long will it take me to go from here to Caerefrog ? How far is it ? Can I get there before the banks close ?"

"Hardly, sir. It's gone one o'clock already, and you won't be able to start much before two. The banks close at three."

"But the staff usually work on until five. How far is it to Caerefrog ?"

"Let's see now. Twenty five miles from here to Prestatyn, and then you follow the coast road for another forty five miles. You turn south for another five—"

"About seventy or eighty miles ? If I start at two, I should be there by half past four at the latest. Right ! I'll ring up the manager and make an appointment. Where's that letter ? Oh, here it is. Caerefrog 631. Come along, Jones ! This is worth another pint. I'm getting somewhere at last. '

12. Banker's Reference

Mr. Iorwerth Prydderch had the bushiest pair of eyebrows that Hopkyn had ever seen. As he bent his head over the letter on his desk, they completely hid his eyes. A very useful appendage for a bank manager, thought Hopkyn, especially when approached for an overdraft, or indeed on such an occasion as this, when the Law, in the shape of a C.I.D. detective, was trying to break through the trad- itional reticence of the Bank.

Mr. Prydderch lifted his head, and a pair of very shrewd grey eyes looked up at Hopkyn.

"Yes, Inspector," he said. "I did write this letter. Or—to be more exact—I dictated it to my secretary, she typed it, and I signed it."

The eyebrows climbed up his forehead, and the grey eyes regarded Hopkyn questioningly.

Hopkyn picked up the letter, folded it, and put it back in his pocket. Mr. Prydderch, he saw, was not the type of witness to volunteer information. This was going to be a difficult interview.

"Did he tell you," began Hopkyn, "why he wished to change his name ?"

Mr. Prydderch half-smiled, and shook his head.

"I have already stated in the letter the only explanation he gave me—for business reasons."

"He didn't say what those reasons were ?"

"No. Nor indeed was it my business to inquire."

Nor yours, he implied.

"You, Inspector," continued Mr. Prydderch, "are probably used to criminals who adopt more names than one. I presume that they invariably do so with fraudulent intent. Legally, however, it is not a crime to assume a different name, or even to use several aliases. A change of name is not a crime unless there is fraudulent intent behind it."

Mr. Prydderch was warming to his topic. Hopkyn, who knew the law about names as well as he did, did not interrupt him. All he wanted was to get the banker to talk, and Mr. Prydderch was now talking.

"My father, Inspector, was a schoolmaster. His name was John Rhydderch Jones, but he was better known by his bardic name, Ap Rhydderch. When I was born, he dropped the Jones from my name, and gave me as surname his bardic name of Ap Rhydderch shortened into Prydderch. Wales, he argued, was too full of Joneses : his children henceforth would be named Prydderch. As I was a minor, there was no need for him to change my name by deed poll. All he did was to enter me on the school register as Iorwerth Prydderch. Usage did the rest."

"It would be an excellent thing if more Joneses followed your father's good example," smiled Hopkyn. "Could it have been the same reason which induced David Beynon to drop the Jones ? He also was a poet."

The shrewd eyes beneath the bushy eyebrows held a glint of amusement. Damn it, said Hopkyn to himself, he knew that I was leading up to that question. A wily old bird !

"Beynon's father knew about my change of name, but I doubt very much whether Beynon did. The change took place thirty years before Beynon was born. He had always known me as Mr. Prydderch. And if he were ignorant of my father's action, he could scarcely have emulated it. David Beynon changed his name for what he described as business reasons. That is all I know, and all I wished to know."

"But it is not a common business practice, is it ?" persisted Hopkyn.

"Common ? No. But on the other hand, neither is it very uncommon. I have several clients on my books who have bought a business and carry it on in the old name."

"But that isn't what Beynon did. He bought an old business and carried on in a new name. Why ?"

"You are very persistent, Inspector. You should know,

being Welsh, that in Wales, where the same surname and often the same Christian name is shared by so many, it is the usual practice to use a double name for identification purposes. In this town, for example, we have at least a hundred Joneses, of whom a good many are David Jones. I'm not sure how many Beynons live here, but there must be a few. In order to distinguish him from the other Davids and the other Beynons, David Beynon was always known by his double name—David Beynon. Whatever were David Beynon's reasons for changing his surname, I was personally not at all surprised that he did so."

"Why ? Just to be out of the common rut ?"

Mr. Prydderch chuckled, dryly.

"You have a most disconcerting habit of barking out questions, Inspector. You make me feel like a hostile witness in a court of law—"

"I beg your pardon, sir. I had no intention of—"

"That's quite all right, Inspector. I suffer from the same proclivity. Usually, however, it is I who do the barking in this room. I am not accustomed to being barked at. It is a most salutary experience."

Hopkyn laughed aloud. He was beginning to like Mr. Iorwerth Prydderch. He decided to put his cards on the table.

"I'm worried, sir," he explained, "and very often worry breeds impatience. Please forgive me if my manner has been offensively abrupt. I was hoping that you would be able to tell me more about David Beynon. You see, I'm trying to find out why he was shot."

The bushy eyebrows shot up the forehead.

"Did you say shot, Inspector ?"

"Yes."

"You mean murdered, not accidentally shot ?"

Hopkyn nodded, and waited.

The Bank Manager pressed the bell on his desk. The door of the office opened, and a young girl stepped into the room.

"Miss Jones," said the Manager, "please tell Mr.

Evans not to wait for me. Ask him to dismiss the staff. You can go too. I don't want to be disturbed."

He waited until the door had closed behind his secretary and again turned to face Hopkyn.

"Sit down, Inspector. I didn't listen-in to the broadcast of the Chairing Ceremony, but there was a very full report of the affair in this morning's *Liverpool Daily Post*. I saw no mention of shooting in that report. On the contrary, the implication was that the Bard had died of heart failure."

A touch of murder, thought Hopkyn, makes the whole world kin. The Bank Manager was too polite to ask questions, but Mrs. Jones Shop Chips could not be more eager for information. The fact that the police had kept the shooting secret made Mr. Prydderch all the more avid to hear about it. The fish is biting, said Hopkyn to himself, I'll give him all the line I've got.

Without more ado, he spun out the yarn. He explained why the police had withheld news of the murder, and then (drawing out his net, as it were) he posed the final question.

"It would help me to discover who shot him if I could find out why he was shot. But I can't find a motive for the murder until I know more about him—his family history, his upbringing, his character, his habits, his life story. That is why I came to see you."

Mr. Prydderch nodded his head, slowly and deliberately.

"Thank you, Inspector," he said at length. "I shall, of course, respect your confidence. Your news has shocked me, and though I had little affection, and less respect, for the character of the deceased, it is nevertheless my duty to place at your disposal all the information concerning him that may help to bring his murderer to justice."

He paused. Very like an old judge, thought Hopkyn, weighing his words very carefully before he begins on his final summing-up. A Victorian old judge, full of flowing cadences.

"I have known David Beynon," continued Mr.

Prydderch, "since the day of his birth. I was very friendly, very friendly indeed, with his late father, Edward Jones. Edward and I were born and bred in the same village, and went to the same village school. We both won scholarships to the County Grammar School, we left that school on the same day, and both of us started our respective careers in the same town—Liverpool : Edward as apprentice in a bookshop, myself as junior clerk in a bank. We shared the same lodgings, and became so attached to each other that when I was transferred to this town four years later, Edward also came here to work."

"At the Book Emporium ?"

"Yes. That was over thirty years ago, Inspector, when we were both young men. It was a very small shop in those days, but Edward worked hard and the business prospered. When the First World War broke out in 1914, I joined up. Edward suffered from a weak heart, and had to stay at home. I was one of the fortunate few who went through the war without a scratch, and in 1919 I came back to Caerefrog. Edward and I, both of us bachelors, again shared the same lodgings. Three years later, in 1922, I was transferred to our branch at Llangollen, and once again Edward and I were separated. We corresponded regularly, and in every letter Edward complained of loneliness. I was more fortunate, because at Llangollen I met the lady who later became my wife. Edward was my best man, and at the reception my wife made a wager with him that he too would soon follow my example."

"She won her bet ?"

"Yes. By that time, Edward had become part-owner of the shop. In 1923, his partner died, and the following year Edward married his dead partner's widow, a lady rather older than himself. Edward, like myself, was then thirty-two, Mrs. Cadwaladr was thirty-seven, but looked younger. She had a boy, Emlyn, who was then seventeen years of age, and I have always believed, Inspector, that it was really for the son's sake that Edward married the mother. Emlyn was the type of boy that Edward had been at his age, and a considerable attachment had sprung up between the two. They used to spend hours together in the shop, arguing about books, discussing poetry, quarrelling about *cynghanedd*. Emlyn Cadwaladr was a precocious youth, and despite the disparity in their ages, he and Edward were twin souls. Then there happened something which might have caused a serious rift between them. Mrs. Cadwaladr, much to her delighted surprise, gave birth to another boy. Edward's cup was now full to overflowing : a child of his own had been added unto Emlyn."

"You said that it *might* have caused a rift in the family. It didn't ?"

"No. Emlyn was now eighteen years of age, and a young man of that age is not vastly concerned with new-born babies. Indeed, Emlyn had already mapped out his future career, and was too busy preparing himself for the University to worry about his baby brother, or half-brother rather. The mother, of course, was overjoyed. The belated unexpectedness of the birth multiplied her joy. The new baby became the hub of her existence. Emlyn being old enough to look after himself, she devoted her whole attention to the new arrival, David Beynon."

"What happened to Emlyn afterwards ?"

"He went to Cardiff University College, and left with an excellent arts degree in 1928 to join the staff of the *Western Mail*. Then, following the plan he had made out for himself, he became a sub-editor of one of the London dailies in 1938. When war again broke out in 1939, he joined the R.A.F., was shot down over Dunkirk, rescued by a destroyer, came home with a bullet in his leg, and was discharged from the services. When he recovered the use of his leg, he again joined up—this time as a War Correspondent. When the war ended, he went to America, and I lost touch with him. His mother told me some time later that he was in Korea covering the war there for the *Chicago Tribune*. And then, early last November, came the cable reporting his death. He had been flying over the enemy lines, and his plane had been shot into the sea. Only the navigator was saved. Emlyn, and the rest of the crew, were drowned."

"Thank you, Mr. Prydderch. You have given me a very clear picture of the family background. To all intents and purposes, David Beynon was an only child?"

"That is so. He was the spoilt darling of a doting mother. When I returned here as Manager of this branch of the Bank, I could see that Edward was worried on his account, but had been too long a bachelor to assert himself as a father. With wiser guidance and firmer discipline, I think the child could have become a credit to his parents. He had a sharp mind, and was quite a lovable boy at times. He had a natural charm which, when he cared to exert it, gained him many friends. Unfortunately, however, the sharpness of his mind turned to cunning, and his charm gained him the wrong friends. When he left school, without having passed his Certificate Examination, Edward asked me if I could find him a job in our bank. For the father's sake, I did so, and David Beynon was appointed junior clerk at one of our Manchester branches. He was then seventeen years of age. Here again he made friends with the wrong people— a fast set of young men and women with far more money to spend than he had. His mother kept him well supplied with pocket-money, but it was not enough for him, and the inevitable happened."

"He embezzled money from the Bank?"

"Yes. Edward reimbursed the Bank, and there was no legal prosecution. David Beynon came home, and was soon afterwards called up for national service. We hoped that two years in the Army would do him some good. What he needed was discipline, and we hoped that the Army would supply it. Our hopes were not fulfilled. The war was over, and Army discipline was not what it had been. Instead of coming home on leave, David Beynon spent it in London, stayed at an expensive hotel, and tried to leave without paying his bill. He was arrested, but Edward again stepped into the breach, and was able to smooth things over. Then there was more trouble over a girl who threatened to bring a breach-of-promise case—"

"This is the first time you have mentioned women," cut in Hopkyn. "Was Beynon equally profligate in that respect ?"

Damn, he thought, I'm getting to talk like him. There must be something infectious in his flowing cadences. Is that why so many of the Victorian novelists wrote in the same vein ?

Mr. Prydderch had both elbows on the desk, the tips of his fingers touching, and his two thumbs slowly and methodically revolving round each other.

"I do not indulge in modern slang, Inspector," he continued, "but there is one word which exactly fits David Beynon. That word is sissy. He lacked the virility of a sexual profligate. He was fond of the company of women, but he liked them in the mass, not individually. His lust was social, not physical. If there is such a word as sissyful, it would very aptly describe both his philosophy and his habits."

"You mean that he liked to show off to women ?"

"To everybody, women especially. It was the result of his mother's infatuation, the fruition of her foolishness. When he was a baby, she dressed him with the sole aim of attracting attention to his beauty. When he began to talk, she bored all her acquaintances with eulogies to his precocity. He was brought up in an atmosphere where it was natural for him to regard himself as the cynosure of all eyes. He showed off, as you very tersely put it, because it was expected of him, and he had been trained to do so. Do I make myself explicit, Inspector ?"

"Remarkably so. But what of his father ? Couldn't he have asserted himself ?"

"Edward was not the stuff of which heavy fathers are made. He had been too long a bachelor to adapt himself to the demands of fatherhood. He could see what was going on, but he was too much of a bookworm to fight against it. He worried himself ill, and died of a broken heart, four years ago. David Beynon was discharged from the army, and came home to help his mother to keep the business going. But a bookshop was not his *metier*. He was of the type who wants to get rich quick, and when his mother died, he sold the business and bought The Wayside Inn, a place more in keeping with his temperament. I have never lost a customer with so much satisfaction. Is there anything else you would like to know, Inspector ?"

Hopkyn smiled.

"You have been an ideal witness," he said, "and I am very glad that I came to see you. I have only one question more. Did David Beynon inherit everything when his mother died ?"

"He did."

"Was his half-brother completely ignored in the mother's will ?"

"Let me explain, Inspector. Edward, as I said, married his dead partner's widow, and the business became their joint property. When Edward died, she inherited everything. The cable reporting Emlyn's death arrived early in November. The sudden shock affected her mind, and she had a slight stroke. No scoundrel is wholly bad, and I must say that David Beynon, during his mother's illness, showed a curious streak of goodness. He spent several hours every day by her bedside, talking and reading to her. In her doting eyes, he was more than ever her white-headed boy. He may have acted thus out of some latent goodness lurking in the depths of his heart, or . . . No ! Let us at least give him the benefit of the doubt, and hope that his solicitude had no ulterior motive. He knew, of course, that his mother had not long to live. So did she. I used to visit her occasionally, and on one of my visits she asked me to write her last will and testament, leaving everything to David. I did so, hoping against hope that he would settle down to his responsibilities when his mother died. He did not. As soon as she was buried, he got a young solicitor to hurry through the probate of the will, and immediately afterwards he sold the business to a rival firm of booksellers."

Mr. Prydderch glanced at the clock on the mantelpiece, and rose. Hopkyn rose with him.

"And now, Inspector, I believe that I have told you everything I know. Mrs. Prydderch always has tea ready at exactly half-past five, and is annoyed if I keep her waiting."

"May I offer you a lift home, sir ?"

"I live on the premises, thank you. I shall show you out, and wish you good afternoon." He chuckled suddenly, a dry cackle that caught Hopkyn by surprise. "If I indulged in sport, Inspector, I might even wish you good hunting."

"I feel most indebted to you," said Hopkyn as he followed the banker to a side door leading out into the street. "But before I go, tell me one thing more. Is there anybody in the bookshop who could give me any further information about David Beynon ? If there is, I feel that I should visit the shop before leaving the town."

"The present manager is Dafydd Parry. He is old, but sharp-witted. He was there when Edward first went there. Edward and Dafydd were very great friends. They thought the world of each other."

"How did Dafydd feel towards the son ?"

"You mean David Beynon ?"

"Yes."

"He detested him. Dafydd's favourite was Emlyn." Mr. Prydderch chuckled again, more dryly than before. "You should by all means have a talk with Dafydd Parry. We live in an age of postage stamps, Inspector : we resemble one another far too closely. The world is losing its characters. Dafydd Parry is one of the few originals left. Good afternoon, Inspector."

"Good afternoon, sir. Thank you very much."

Hopkyn stepped outside, and the door closed behind him. He smiled broadly. So the world is losing its characters, is it ? Well, he had just spent a very profitable half-hour with one of them.

13. Dafydd Parry

The town clock was chiming the half-hour when Hopkyn stood in front of The Book Emporium. The windows were drab and shabby, and there came through the open doorway the musty smell of dusty books. Through the door there came also a lively youth carrying an iron gate, one end of which he fitted into a metal framework in the doorway. He looked up perkily at Hopkyn, as if daring him to enter the shop on the stroke of closing time, and again retreated into the interior, reappearing almost immediately with an iron bar and a padlock. Following hard on his footsteps came a very old man wearing a bowler hat so green with age that nobody would believe it had ever enjoyed any other colour. A black alpaca coat, a canary-coloured waistcoat embroidered in pink, and a shiny pair of black striped trousers completed his ensemble. A long aquiline nose turned in Hopkyn's direction, and two bright blue eyes looked at him over a pair of small steel-framed spectacles.

"Mr. Dafydd Parry ?" inquired Hopkyn.

The blue eyes looked him up and down. A lean forefinger pushed the glasses a little higher on the nose, and Hopkyn found himself being studied through two lenses as thick as microscopes.

Dafydd Parry nodded.

"That is my name," he said. The depth of his voice took Hopkyn by surprise. He had expected a thinner tone from so scraggy a neck. "You have left your business too late, my friend. Time flies, death urges, knells call, heaven invites, hell threatens. Edward Young."

Hopkyn smiled.

"Complete the quotation," he said. "Like our shadows, our wishes lengthen as our sun declines."

The old man craned his neck to have a better look at him.

"Ah !" he nodded. "So you too know your Young, eh ? I had feared that in this whirligig of time he had become an old man's poet—the knell, the shroud, the mattock and the grave ; the deep damp vault, the darkness, and the worm. The shop is closed, my friend, and the boy waits upon my pleasure with the key. Come here tomorrow, young man."

Hopkyn shook his head.

"I shall not keep you long. All I ask is a few minutes' talk."

"Talk. Men talk to conceal the mind. Edward Young again, borrowing this time from old Jeremy Taylor. Before Young was born, Jeremy had said that speech was given to man to conceal his thoughts. So you want to talk to me ? All right, I'll give you ten minutes. Boy !"

The sudden shout startled Hopkyn, but the boy was obviously immured to it.

"Yessir ?"

"Make the gate ready. Padlock the portcullis, but give me the key. Then go home. Stand not upon the order of your going, but go at once."

"Shakespeare, sir."

"Correct. And the play ?"

"Macbeth, sir."

"Correct. Here's your sixpence. Good night, lad."

"Here's the key, sir. I'll fix the padlock ready for you to lock it."

"You forgot to say thank you. How sharper than a serpent's tooth it is to have a thankless child."

"King Lear, sir."

"Correct. Here's another sixpence. That's all you get tonight. Be off with you."

"Thank you, sir. Good night, sir."

Dafydd Parry, chuckling deeply in his throat, led the way into the shop. Hopkyn followed him, smiling.

"A good lad, that," said Dafydd Parry. "I've started him on Shakespeare this year. He'll go far, that boy."

"Is he still at school ?" asked Hopkyn.

"No. He failed to get a scholarship to the Grammar

School because he couldn't get his sums right." The old man snorted. "Sums ! Bacon said that it was mathematics which made men subtle, but that it was histories which made them wise, and poets which made them witty. That little lad will learn more in my shop than in any school."

"He certainly will," chuckled Hopkyn, "at sixpence a quotation."

"Shakespeare will stay with him when the sixpences are spent. Here we are. Sit ye down, and tell me what you want. Speak right out."

"Julius Caesar. Do I collect a sixpence ?"

"No. I'll give you an extra five minutes. You want some information about books ?"

"Information, yes. About books, no."

"Oh ! Who sent you ?"

"Mr. Iorwerth Prydderch."

The bright blue eyes looked hard at Hopkyn.

"Hm. The banker, eh ? It can't be about money, because I've got none. And it can't be about books, because he reads none. The only thing we had in common was a friend. Wait ! I think I can guess what you want. Are you a detective ?"

"Yes."

"Name ?"

"Detective Inspector Hopkyn, Scotland Yard."

"The rank is but the guinea's stamp. I don't hold with the absurd practice of addressing people by their occupation. Why should I be expected to say Doctor Jones or Professor Hughes or Detective Inspector Hopkyn, when I am not expected to say Greengrocer Griffiths or Tailor Thomas or Chartered Accountant Charles ? I shall call you Mr. Hopkyn."

Hopkyn laughed.

"When you first addressed me, you called me friend. I liked it."

"I give every man friendship, let him spurn it who will."

"Did David Beynon spurn it ?"

Dafydd Parry pushed the small lenses up his nose, and Hopkyn once again felt himself under the microscope.

"Ah ! So it's David Beynon you wish to talk about, eh ? The Chair Bard who died so suddenly yesterday ?"

"Yes."

The old man looked up at Hopkyn, quizzically.

"The lady was not for burning," he quoted, and added, with a sardonic chuckle, "Nor the bard for chairing, eh ? How should I know why he died of a weak heart ? I didn't even know that he had a heart. I found him a most heartless little scamp. Go and see his doctor. I don't want to talk about him."

"Did you listen-in to the Chairing Ceremony ?"

"No. I never listen-in. Broadcasting may be an excellent way of passing the time for illiterates, but I can read."

"You read the newspaper accounts of his death ?"

"I did."

The old man was becoming a hostile witness, felt Hopkyn. I'm making heavy weather of this interview. How can I improve the going ?

"Have you read the Chair Ode ?"

"Not yet. The books will not arrive here from the printers until tomorrow."

"Knowing the poet, I suppose you'll read the Chair Ode with special interest ?"

"Knowing the poet, Mr. Hopkyn, I shall read the Ode with very special interest, if only to discover who the devil did write it."

"I see. You don't think that David Beynon himself could have written it ?"

"Think ? I know he couldn't. Somebody wrote it for him."

"For money ?"

"What else ? Don't look so shocked, man. I can name you half a dozen so-called poets in this very town who are Chaired Bards because they paid a poet for writing the odes which won them their Chairs." Dafydd Parry cackled loudly. "An old friend of mine, Eryr Gwynedd—

God rest his bones !—won dozens of Chairs for his customers. When he died, seventeen local poets died with him."

"Surely," objected Hopkyn, "you don't rate the National Eisteddfod so cheaply ? What you have said may be true of small village eisteddfodau. But no poet would sacrifice the honour of winning the National Eisteddfod Chair—"

"What is honour ?" interrupted Dafydd Parry. "A word. What is that word, honour ? Air. A trim reckoning. Who hath it ? He that died o' Wednesday." Another dry cackle. "Falstaff was a day out. David Beynon died on a Thursday. No, no, no, Mr. Hopkyn ! Whoever wrote the Chair Ode this year, I give you my word that it wasn't David Beynon !"

"I understand that he was very fond of reading poetry, and reciting it ?"

"Fond ?" The old man's brow wrinkled in thought. "Studious of ease and fond of humble things. Who said that ? Was it John Philips ?"

"No. Ambrose Philips."

"Ah ! You're right. From Holland to a Friend in England—that's the poem, isn't it ? David Beynon was neither studious nor fond of humble things. He loved the gaudy and the bawdy, his taste was low and his knowledge scanty. He was one of those who had been at a great feast of languages, and stolen the scraps. Love's Labour's Lost."

This tack was leading nowhere, thought Hopkyn. I'll try another.

"Mr. Prydderch seemed to share your opinion of David Beynon. But he spoke in much higher terms of his half-brother."

"Emlyn ?"

That's better, said Hopkyn to himself. I've touched the right spot at last. There's a new twinkle in the old man's eyes and a new ring to his voice.

"A Corinthian, a lad of mettle, a good boy. Emlyn had a large and fruitful mind. Bacon. I remember him coming here as a boy, on holiday from school. He'd settle himself down in that corner by the window, and he'd stay there all day browsing in a book. I've watched him put the book down now and then, and think over it, digesting it bit by bit until he'd absorbed the whole of it. D'ye remember what Michael Drayton wrote of Henry Reynolds ? Nor that fine madness still he did retain, which rightly should possess a poet's brain. Aye, I'd say to myself looking at him, that boy has a brain, he's a thinker. Beware when the great God lets loose a thinker on this planet, said Emerson. But I knew, even then, that here was a thinker whom the world would have to listen to one day."

"A bloom whose petals, nipped before they blew, died on the promise of the fruit," murmured Hopkyn—and stopped suddenly when he saw the old man staring at him.

"What's that got to do with it ?" barked Dafydd Parry.

"Surely," said Hopkyn, "you recognise the quotation ?"

"Of course I do," snapped Dafydd. "It's from Shelley's epitaph to Keats. But what's the point of quoting it now?"

It was Hopkyn's turn to look puzzled.

"Mr. Prydderch told me," he explained, "that Emlyn was killed last November. That is what made me think of Keats, another poet who died young."

The old man sat back, and nodded his head slowly.

"I see," he said. "Yes, yes, we all thought he was dead. But the report wasn't true. The Communists rescued him, kept him a prisoner for eight months, treated him very well, and then unexpectedly released him, probably hoping that he'd tell everybody how kind they are to their prisoners. Didn't you read about it in the papers ?"

"No, I've no recollection of . . ."

"You must have. The *Daily Express* made a front-page splash of it last Saturday—*Lynd Waller Released from Communist Prison Camp* !"

"Lynd Waller ?" asked Hopkyn. "You mean the American journalist ?"

"Yes."

"Do you mean to tell me that Emlyn Cadwaladr and Lynd Waller are one and the same man ?"

"That's right. Emlyn Cadwaladr was too big a mouthful for the Yanks, so he shortened it to Lynd Waller. He ..."

The old man stopped short, and gazed questioningly at Hopkyn.

"What's worrying you ?"

"Mr. Prydderch didn't know that Emlyn was alive. But he must have read the story of his release from the prison camp. Didn't he know that Lynd Waller was Emlyn ?"

"Why should he ? They lost touch when Emlyn went to America. I was the only one who corresponded with him. Prydderch and Emlyn hadn't got much in common."

"And you had ?"

"Yes. He came here to see me on Monday ..."

"This week ?"

"Yes. Last Monday. I'd gone away to a book auction, and wouldn't be back until late on Tuesday. So he left a note for me. Wait a minute ! I've still got it. Yes, here it is. Read it."

Hopkyn read the scribbled note.

Dear Old friend :
You've already seen in the papers that the report of my death was as exaggerated as that of Mark Twain. Sorry I missed you today. Never mind. I'm off to the Eisteddfod, and intend staying the week there. See you next Monday. Can you put me up for a few days ?

Love,

EMLYN.

Hopkyn folded the note, and returned it. Several questions were buzzing through his head.

"You said you were the only one in this town he corresponded with. What about David Beynon ? Did they write to each other ?"

Dafydd Parry shook his head.

"No. Emlyn had left College when David Beynon was a baby in arms. And when Emlyn joined the R.A.F. in 1939, David Beynon was still in school."

"You said Emlyn went to the States five years ago. Did he come home for his father's funeral ?"

"Emlyn was in Korea when his father died. He couldn't have come home in time for the funeral."

"Did David Beynon know that Emlyn's pen-name was Lynd Waller ?"

"I don't think so. His mother didn't. Emlyn never talked to anybody about his writing, except to me."

The old man was getting restive. The cross-examination was trying his patience. He glared at Hopkyn through his thick lenses.

"What are all these questions leading up to ?" he demanded. "Be blunt, man ! Stop beating about the bush !"

"Very well," said Hopkyn. "I'll be blunt, very blunt. You say that David Beynon could not have written the Chair Ode. But Emlyn Cadwaladr could have written it, couldn't he ? No, wait ! Let me finish. In the note I have just read, Emlyn says that he was going to the Eisteddfod. David Beynon died there yesterday. Emlyn probably saw him die. Even if he wasn't inside the pavilion at the time, he must have known before evening that his half-brother was dead. Why didn't he come forward ? Why did he lurk in the background ? Can *you* tell me ?"

The old man sat up, tense and combative.

"Yes, I'll tell you ! Of all the—"

Hopkyn again halted him.

"Dafydd Parry," he said quietly, "you'll understand why I am asking you these questions when I tell you that David Beynon did not die a natural death. He was shot through the heart."

The old man stared at him, uncomprehendingly, for a second or two. Hopkyn felt a pang of sympathy for him as he sank back in his chair, all his combativeness gone.

"Shot ?" he whispered. "You mean that he was murdered ?"

Hopkyn nodded without speaking. Dafydd Parry breathed deeply. He's aged five years in as many seconds, thought Hopkyn. Poor old fellow !

Neither spoke for a minute. Then the old man drew his tongue along his dry lips, and again spoke, slowly and quietly.

"It wasn't Emlyn who shot him."

"I'm not suggesting it was," said Hopkyn.

"No, but I know how your mind works. And oft, though wisdom wake, said Milton, suspicion sleeps at Wisdom's gate, and to simplicity resigns her charge." Another long pause. "And to simplicity resigns her charge." The quiet voice gained confidence. "No, my friend, it wasn't Emlyn Cadwaladr. Emlyn isn't a murderer. You must not let your wisdom resign her charge to simplicity. You are wrong, wrong, wrong !"

"You didn't complete the quotation, Dafydd Parry. Shall I do so ? And to simplicity resigns her charge, while goodness thinks no ill where no ill seems. You are a good friend, Dafydd Parry, a good friend who can see no ill. But in my job, I must not be satisfied with how things seem. I have to get at the truth. If Emlyn is innocent—"

"I know he is !"

"Then he has nothing to fear. Nor have you, Dafydd Parry. It is consciousness of guilt that makes cowards of us all. Shall I tell Emlyn that you wish to be remembered to him ?"

Dafydd Parry nodded. Hopkyn rose, and offered him his hand. The old man did not see it. He was staring at the corner where Emlyn used to sit as a boy. Hopkyn turned on his heels, and walked quietly through the corridors of books. He turned at the door, and looked back at the old man. Dafydd Parry had not moved. He looked old, and unutterably sad.

Hopkyn stepped out, and closed the door quietly behind him.

14. Emlyn Cadwaladr

Hopkyn looked out through his bedroom window. It was a glorious summer morning. Rhyd-yr-Onnen had been very lucky : the fine weather which had held all week had drawn enormous crowds to the Eisteddfod, and this morning promised another record attendance for the last day.

The door opened and the Chief bustled in.

"Morning, Hopkyn. Coming down for breakfast ?"

"Hello, Chief. You're a very early bird this morning."

"Wanted to locate that fellow Cadwaladr," explained the Chief. "It was a very smart piece of work you did yesterday, Hopkyn. We'll have him under lock and key before lunch, I hope. He's staying at The Blue Lion."

"Under what name ?" asked Hopkyn. "His own, or Lynd Waller ?"

"Emlyn Cadwaladr," replied the Chief. "He'd booked a bed sitting-room for the whole week, spends the morning writing in his room, and the rest of the day at the Eisteddfod. Got a season ticket, the manager told me. When shall we go and see him ?"

"Straight after breakfast. The sooner the better."

"He must have the nerve of the devil to stay out the week here."

Hopkyn shook his head.

"It would be far more risky for him to leave, Chief. He must be wondering at this moment why we have concealed the shooting. What are we up to ? He doesn't know, but he's going to take particular care that he'll do nothing to attract attention. A season ticket holder who suddenly quits the Eisteddfod leaves an empty seat to mark his absence. And in a crowded pavilion, an empty seat might lead to comment. No, Chief, he's far too clever to run so obvious a risk."

"Come on, Hopkyn," said the Chief, impatiently.

"Let's get breakfast over and have it out with him. I'm getting jittery. If we leave it too late and find the bird flown, there will be hell to pay."

"No fear of that," smiled Hopkyn. "Lynd Waller is too well-known a journalist to hide himself for long. All right, Chief, I'm coming."

Half an hour later, the manager of the Blue Lion was leading them to Emlyn Cadwaladr's room.

"We'll introduce ourselves, Mr. Davies," said the Chief.

"Thank you."

The manager hesitated, full of curiosity. The Chief eyed him coldly.

"We needn't detain you any longer," he said. "Our business with Mr. Cadwaladr is private. If necessary, we'll see you later."

The manager mumbled a reply which sounded apologetic, and left them. The Chief knocked on the door, opened it, and he and Hopkyn stepped inside.

Emlyn Cadwaladr was writing, and looked up with a frown of irritation. The Chief closed the door, and stood with his back to it.

"Mr. Emlyn Cadwaladr ?" he asked.

Emlyn nodded, and eyed them in turn.

"You have the advantage of me," he said. "I know that you are the Chief Constable, but I don't know your friend. Is he also a policeman ? He's big enough."

"Detective Inspector Hopkyn, of Scotland Yard."

"So. And your business with me ?"

"We want to ask you a few questions, Mr. Cadwaladr," said Hopkyn. "I think you can guess their nature."

Emlyn smiled noncommittally.

"I am afraid that I'm rather too busy, Inspector, to indulge in guessing-games. It would save time if you asked your questions forthwith."

The Chief glared, and Hopkyn chuckled.

"Cut the cackle, Hopkyn," barked the Chief. "Get down to business."

"It might also save time, Mr. Cadwaladr, both yours and ours," said Hopkyn, "if I first of all told you what we already know about you. You can correct me if I am wrong. You were born in 1907, and lost your father when you were 16 years old. Your mother afterwards married your late father's partner, and gave birth to a son, your half-brother David Beynon, in 1925. You went to Cardiff University College, joined the staff of the *Western Mail* in 1928, became sub-editor of a London daily in 1937, joined the R.A.F. in 1939, were discharged in 1941, became a war correspondent, and went to America when the war ended. You were appointed Foreign Correspondent of the *Chicago Tribune*, and adopted the pen-name of Lynd Waller. In 1946, you were sent out to cover the war in Korea. Am I right?"

"Remarkably so."

"In November, your plane was shot down over enemy lines, and you were reported dead. The Communists rescued and imprisoned you, released you last month, and you landed in this country last Saturday."

Hopkyn paused. Emlyn Cadwaladr put his hand in his coat pocket, and the Chief made ready to pounce. He relaxed when Emlyn's hand reappeared with a cigarette case. Emlyn took out a cigarette, lit it, and waited. The silence grew.

"Well?" barked the Chief.

"Very well, thank you," said Emlyn, smiling gravely at him. "But I'm still waiting for your questions, and my time is valuable."

The Chief's face reddened, and Hopkyn hurried on.

"Mr. Cadwaladr, were you at the Eisteddfod on Thursday afternoon, watching the Chairing Ceremony?"

"I was."

"Did you recognise the Chair Bard?"

"I did."

"He was your brother?"

"My half-brother."

"I beg your pardon. Had you also competed for the Chair?"

Emlyn again smiled.

"That is a question which is never asked at the Eistedfod, Inspector. Nobody is unkind enough to ask an unsuccessful competitor if he is among the losers."

"I am the exception who asks, Mr. Cadwaladr. I repeat the question. Did you compete for the Chair ?"

"I intended to."

"You have been to Malaya, I believe ?"

"I have."

"You have had experience of jungle warfare there ?"

"As a correspondent, yes."

"As a correspondent in the front line with the troops ?"

"That is so."

"Had your brother—I beg your pardon, your half-brother—had he any experience of jungle warfare ?"

"I don't think so."

The Chief could stand it no longer.

"For Heaven's sake, Hopkyn," he exploded, "ask him plainly and bluntly if it was he who wrote the damn poem !"

Emlyn's smile broadened.

"Thank you, Chief," he said. "A plain question deserves a plain answer. Yes, it was I who wrote the damn poem."

"But it was your half-brother who got the Chair ?"

Emlyn chuckled, dryly.

"Did he get it ?"

The Chief snorted.

"You're splitting hairs, Hopkyn ! Look here, Cadwaladr, tell us the unvarnished truth. You wrote the poem. Then you were reported dead. So your half-brother sent your poem to the Eisteddfod in his own name and won the Chair with it. That's the plain truth, isn't it ?"

The smile left Emlyn's face. Hopkyn saw his fingers tighten on the cigarette until it bent and split. The Chief's blunt speaking had touched him on the raw.

"You're right," he said. "The damned scoundrel won the Chair with my poem. May his soul rot in hell ! I was there looking at him strutting on to the stage like a peacock, beaming all over his face like a bloody nancy

III

boy, delighted with the whole thing, revelling in the adulation of the crowd. And then—suddenly—he saw me sitting there, looking at him, and the smile was wiped off his face. He knew what was coming to him." He paused, threw away the broken cigarette, and took out another. Then he said, quietly and slowly, "I'm glad he died. He deserved to die."

The Chief looked at Hopkyn, and nodded.

"One more question, Mr. Cadwaladr," said Hopkyn. "Nobody heard the shot, nobody saw the flash of the gun. How did you shoot him ?"

Emlyn was lighting another cigarette when Hopkyn put the question to him. The match slipped through his fingers, and he stared blankly at the detective.

"How did I shoot him ?" he repeated. "I didn't shoot him !"

"Man alive !" cried the Chief. "You've just confessed to it !"

"Don't be absurd ! I've confessed to no such thing ! How the devil can I confess to something that I know nothing about ?"

"You told us just now," said Hopkyn quietly, "that Beynon saw you looking at him, and that he knew then what was coming to him. What came to him was death by shooting. Isn't that what you meant ?"

Emlyn drew a deep breath.

"No ! What I meant was that as soon as he saw me there, he knew that I'd expose him. I could easily prove that the poem was mine, and that he had stolen it. I was waiting for the shouting to die down before getting up on my feet to accuse him. But when he collapsed, there was nothing I could do. And when I heard afterwards that he was dead, I thought that it was the shock of seeing me sitting there, alive, looking at him, that killed him. I know nothing about the shooting."

"Why didn't you come forward when you heard of his death ?"

"Why should I ? I didn't want anything to do with him."

"Were you still going to expose him and to claim the Chair ?"

"Of course I was. But there was no particular hurry, now that he was dead. I decided to talk it over with Dafydd Parry, and be guided by his advice. Dafydd Parry is—"

"I've seen Dafydd Parry. I had a long interview with him yesterday," said Hopkyn. "Tell me, when did you first learn that your half-brother had won the Chair ?"

"When I saw him escorted to the stage. I knew it was my poem when the adjudicator quoted from it. I had sent it to Dafydd Parry on the morning of the day I was shot down and taken prisoner. Dafydd can confirm that it is my poem."

"Why send it to Dafydd Parry ?"

"I wanted Dafydd to read it before I sent it to the Eisteddfod. I hadn't written any poetry for a long long time, and I was afraid the *cynghanedd* was a bit rusty."

Hopkyn nodded, and turned to the Chief.

"I can see what happened, Chief. The poem was sent by ordinary mail. The report of the death was cabled, and arrived before the poem. You had addressed the poem to Dafydd Parry at the shop, I presume ?"

"Yes, I used the shop address."

"Beynon recognised your handwriting, and opened the package, knowing you were dead. The cable reporting your death had been sent to your mother, of course, as next of kin ?"

"Yes."

"Beynon had seen the cable, and when your poem arrived, he thought it was quite safe to steal it. He kept it until he went to the Wayside Inn, typed three copies of it, and sent them in his own name to the competition. But there's one thing I don't understand, Mr. Cadwaladr."

He paused.

"Yes ?"

"Dafydd Parry showed me the note you had written to him on Monday. There was no mention of the poem in the note. You didn't even ask if he'd received the poem. Why not ?"

"There was no point in asking him about it. It was much too late to enter the poem for the competition. We'd discuss it, of course, when we met, but—"

"Didn't you think that Dafydd Parry might have sent the poem in your name to the Eisteddfod ?"

"Without my permission ? No, no ! He'd never have done it !"

Hopkyn tried another tack.

"You have a season ticket to the Eisteddfod, Mr. Cadwaladr, haven't you ? May I see it, please ?"

Emlyn produced the ticket, and handed it over.

"Block B, Row E, Seat 17," read Hopkyn. "If I remember correctly, Block B is the centre block of front seats, and Row E would be the fifth row of seats in that block. The seats are numbered from the left, and you would be sitting to the left of your brother when he was shot."

"Is that important ?"

"Yes. It was the direction the bullet came from."

"Oh."

"Your seat was Number 17. Were seats 16 and 18 occupied at that time ?"

"You mean during the Chairing Ceremony ?"

"Yes."

Emlyn nodded.

"The doors were shut at half-past two, and both seats were occupied. A young girl, about twenty-four or twenty-five years of age, sat on my left hand in seat 18, and her husband sat on her left, in seat 19. My right-hand neighbour was an elderly gentleman wearing a clerical collar."

"Did you know any of them ?"

"No."

"Did you get to know them ?"

"The old gentleman told me his name was Jones, but that isn't very helpful, is it ? I overheard the husband calling his wife Dilys, and she called him Tom. These two had a season ticket each, and came to the Eisteddfod for some part of every session. The old gentleman's seat was sometimes occupied by an elderly lady, probably his wife. They must have shared the one ticket."

"We can check up on the seats," said Hopkyn. "That's all, I think, Mr. Cadwaladr. I'm sorry we've taken up so much of your time, but I'm sure you can appreciate now why we had to do it."

Emlyn got up.

"The apologies should come from me, Inspector. I'm sorry that I was so abrupt with you both when you first came in. Please forgive me."

The Chief did not feel at all satisfied. He had been so convinced of Emlyn's guilt that this sudden *volte-face* of Hopkyn's left him perturbed and uneasy.

"We may have to see you again, Mr. Cadwaladr," he grunted. "When do you propose leaving here?"

"I shall be here until Monday morning," replied Emlyn. "I'm going to see Dafydd Parry on Monday, and I shall probably stay at Caerefrog for a few days."

"Right. We'll contact you if necessary. Good morning."

PART TWO

THE MURDERER

The General Secretary of the Eisteddfod awoke, yawned, stretched himself, and looked at the clock on the mantelpiece. It was half-past six.

Good, he said to himself. Another half-hour in bed.

He reached for the cigarette-case and the lighter lying ready on the bedside table, lit a cigarette, and inhaled deeply. This first smoke of the day had an ecstasy that was all its own. Sometimes, but not very often, he overslept, and then the first morning smoke became so hurried a rite that it only slaked his desire. Today, however, he could take his time over it, enjoying it to the full.

It had been a good, busy, satisfying week. The Treasurer had confidentially informed him that the financial success of the Eisteddfod was already assured : the takings for Friday and Saturday would be clear profit. All the press reports had spoken well of the smooth working of the Eisteddfod ; and Mr. John Phillips, the gifted young Secretary, had been extolled in all the papers for his organising ability—"The Eisteddfod Council," suggested one editorial, "would be well advised to consider the advisability of appointing this talented young man as a permanent secretary."

Phillips felt very pleased with himself. Refreshed in mind and body by a good night's rest, he was more than ready to face the last day of the Eisteddfod.

Sometime, somewhere, he had read that a murderer could not sleep. Was it Lady Macbeth who had said something about murder killing sleep ? He couldn't remember. Never took much interest in literature. Anyway, it wasn't true. Murdering Beynon had not cost him an hour's sleep.

He looked at the hand holding the cigarette. Not a tremor. No sign of nerves. There had been one moment on Thursday, though, when his nerve nearly broke. But he couldn't have helped it. He had planned everything very very carefully, but the sudden advent of a Scotland Yard detective was a contingency he could not have foreseen. He had realised, of course, that a detective would be called in sooner or later, but he hadn't expected one to arrive so promptly. Gave him a turn. But everything had worked out all right, and he smiled when he remembered that it was the detective himself who had restored his calmness, who had given him a whisky and a homily to help pull himself together. He had kept unobtrusively in the background during the conference with Hopkyn and the Chief Constable at the hospital. Fortunately, that old fool William, that elephantine ass of a Chairman, had occupied most of the stage. Since that interview, he hadn't seen the detective. He had made tentative inquiries about him on Friday morning, and had been told that Hopkyn had gone away for the day.

He'll probably come to see me today, he said to himself. All right. Let him. There's nothing he can do. I suppose I shall be called to give evidence at the inquest on Monday morning. No snags there. I'll just corroborate what Dr. Lloyd says. I shall also have to attend the funeral. Who's arranging it, I wonder? Not my business. But the Committee will want me to buy a wreath. I'll get William to do that : he'll love it.

Yes, it had been a good week, a very good week. I wish, though, that I could have told Beynon that I was going to kill him. And especially to explain to him why I had to kill him. But anyway, if there's any truth in the story of survival after death, he should know by now why he died.

1. Brother and Sister

John Phillips and his twin sister Nancy were born at Bootle, Liverpool, in 1926. Their father was a Liverpool Welshman, their mother an Anglesey woman, and the language of their home was Welsh.

When War broke out in 1939, John and Nancy were evacuated to their grandmother's home in Anglesey. Two years later, during the nine nights' blitz on Liverpool, both their parents were killed.

Granny Williams, as they called her, was a widow. She was the village postmistress. The Post Office occupied only a corner of her shop. The rest of the premises was crammed with such a rich assortment of merchandise that she herself never knew for certain what she had in stock. Nancy, always full of curiosity, had one day climbed up a step-ladder to see what lay behind the stacked boxes of soap-powder that lined the front of the shelf above the shop door. She found half-a-dozen coloured mugs for Queen Victoria's Jubilee, a box of long black gloves used for funerals fifty years ago, a dozen penholders strung on a piece of cardboard, two pairs of black shoes with elastic sides, and—most glorious find of all in war-time—three packets of loaf sugar.

Postal Orders, smoked herrings, stamps, stationery, liquorice allsorts, bootlaces, tin kettles—Granny Williams sold them all, and much else besides. The villagers, after spending a fruitless day searching the big shops at Holyhead and Bangor, often returned home to find what they sought at Granny's little shop.

She struggled hard to educate the two children. Neither of them was particularly bright, but both managed to scrape through the Scholarship Examination to the County School. Nancy failed to matriculate, and spent an extra year at school learning shorthand and typewriting. John passed, with honours in Applied

Mathematics, but had no desire for a University career. He had decided to become a teacher, specialising in Handwork.

In 1944, when he was eighteen years of age, John was called up for his National Service. Nancy had persuaded Granny Williams to send her for a year's training at a Commercial College in Liverpool, and was now short-hand-typist with a firm of brokers. She hated the work, hated the office, hated the monotony of having to live in cheap lodgings and wear drab clothes.

And then, quite suddenly, Granny Williams died. Robert Owen Greengrocer, who hadn't slept a wink since Saturday because he had an all-correct line in his Penny Points Football Pool, was on Monday morning standing on the doorstep of the shop waiting for Granny Williams to open it. The rules stated that any client with an all-correct line must send in his claim by telegram on Monday, and the shilling for the telegram was already burning a hole in Robert's pocket. When his watch showed that it was ten minutes past nine, his impatience could be curbed no longer. He knocked loudly on the shop door. There was no reply. He knocked louder. Still no reply. Robert Owen swore under his breath, and being a deacon in the chapel, looked furtively around in case someone had heard him. He then went round to the back door of the house. The milkman had already been, and the bottle was still on the doorstep.

"Never known her to sleep late before," he muttered, and tried the door.

It was locked.

It was only then that Robert thought something might have happened to the old lady. He jumped over the low wall into the garden next door, and had a hurried colloquy with Old Martha, the next door neighbour. Her son Jim, an insurance agent, had not yet started on his morning round. Robert and Jim, having failed to get a response to their continued knocking, broke a pane in Granny's kitchen window, and climbed in.

The table had been laid for breakfast, and there was an unlit fire in the grate. But of Granny, not a sign.

They called her name, but she did not answer. Martha had joined them by now, and she led the way upstairs. The two men waited on the landing, and Martha entered the bedroom. She called to them.

Old Granny Williams was sleeping so peacefully that they did not at first realise that she was dead.

The little village gave her a grand funeral. When it was over, Mr. Prysor, the solicitor from Llangefni, had a private talk with Nancy and John. The old lady, he told them, had known for a long time that her heart was weak, and that the end might come unawares. But she refused to make a fuss about it. The only effect it had had upon her was that every night, before she went to bed, she made everything spick and span for the morning, in case other eyes than hers would inspect the kitchen.

Her last will and testament had been drawn up by Mr. Prysor himself, in his own handwriting. Granny had insisted on that.

"None of that machine writing," she had said, "I've seen too many quarrels about wills, and I want you to write mine in your own hand, so that nobody can say there was any hanky-panky. The silver teapot and the tray on the sideboard are to go to my cousin Mary's daughter, and you'd better give her ten pounds to buy herself new clothes for the funeral. She'll be going to College soon, so tell her to buy grey, not black. No, make it twenty pounds. Her father's got plenty of brass, but he's a farmer, and a bit stingy with it. I want to leave another twenty pounds to the chapel, too, to buy cushions for the big pew where the deacons sit. It may stop them squirming so much when the preacher is long-winded on a cold night. And here's a list of neighbours who have done me a good turn some time or other. I don't want you to write all these names in my will, but I'd like them to have something to remember me by—a teapot or a jam-dish or something. But don't let them choose for themselves, or Old Martha Next Door will take something too good for her. I'll write down opposite each name what you should give them, and leave the paper in the big Bible on the chest-of-drawers there. You've got all that clear, now ? Very well. All the rest goes to Nancy and John. Neither of them will come here to live, and my furniture will be too old-fashioned for them when they make their own homes. Tell them to keep something small to remember me by, and then get Mortimer Evans the auctioneer to sell everything, house and all, and put the money in the bank. I've got a little there already, and Mr. Smith the Midland is looking after it for me. Put the whole lot together, and then share it equally between Nancy and John. You're sure you've got all that down ?"

"I'll let you know," said Mr. Prysor to them, "what the estate amounts to, but you mustn't expect too much from the auction sale, though old furniture in good condition commands good prices nowadays. Mr. Smith has already told me that your grandmother's account at the bank is not far short of a thousand pounds."

Nancy gasped aloud.

"You mean that John and I will get nearly five hundred pounds each ?" she asked.

"You'll get more than that," replied Mr. Prysor, "when everything is settled. I cannot, of course, commit myself to a figure just now. It will take some time to settle the estate, but I'll get in touch with you as soon as possible."

John had returned to his army camp, and Nancy to her brokers' office. Both of them had loved their granny, and Nancy had wept copious tears at the graveside. She was more volatile than John, more demonstrative, more superficial. John felt not only his granny's death, but also the void left by her passing. This was the second home he had lost. There was no third home to go to. Nancy in time would feel the loss more than he, though she now appreciated it less. He could ride a storm, she needed an anchor. She took after their mother, he after their father. The father, a foreman carpenter at Cammel

Lairds, the big ship-builders, had been the quiet steady type on whom you could lean and rest. The mother, a more colourful personality, lacked his steadfastness and reliability. When John and Nancy were children, it was to their mother they ran when they were pleased about something, but to their father when they were in any kind of trouble.

Nancy's grief, as John had foreseen, did not last long. They corresponded regularly, and week by week Nancy's letters dealt more and more with the money coming to them. Why hadn't the solicitors written ? Why didn't Mr. Prysor tell them how much the auction had made ? When were they getting their money ? She was fed up with the brokers' office. She wanted something more lively. A friend of hers was going to open a beauty parlour. She wanted a partner. Didn't John think it a good idea for her to invest her money in the partnership ? Beauty shops made colossal profits.

John counselled caution, spoke of National Savings Certificates and Defence Bonds, tried to explain the difference between capital and income. Nancy was not interested.

The letter from Mr. Prysor arrived when John was on leave from Germany. He and Nancy went to see him, and Mr. Prysor explained to them in great detail how much the estate had realised. John listened attentively, Nancy impatiently. Each left the solicitor's office with a cheque for eight hundred and fifty pounds. To Nancy, it seemed eight million.

Lying in bed, smoking his cigarette, and looking back over the years, John wondered if that cheque had marked the beginning of Nancy's downfall. He had tried hard to persuade her to save the money, but to Nancy money was made for spending. She gave up her office job, spent a glorious week buying all sorts of clothes, and then wrote to tell John that she was investing her money in her friend's beauty parlour. They were going to live in the flat above the shop, and life was going to be marvellous.

John left the Army in August, and entered Bangor

Normal College in September, 1946. At the end of the two years' course, he qualified as a teacher, and was awarded the College Diploma of Distinction in Handwork. He saw an advertisement in the *Schoolmaster* for a Handwork Master at Rhyd-yr-Onnen Secondary Modern School, applied for the post, was appointed, and commenced duties there in September, 1948.

The Modern School at Rhyd-yr-Onnen was a new school. All the Junior Schools within a radius of twenty miles contributed pupils to it. At eleven years of age, all children in the Junior Schools had to sit what was officially called the Schools' Examination, but was locally known as The Scholarship. Those who passed The Scholarship were sent to the Rhyd-yr-Onnen Grammar School, those who failed to the Rhyd-yr-Onnen Modern School. As there were always more failures than passes, the Modern School was a much bigger school than the Grammar School. Its pupils entered it with a natural feeling of frustration : they had come there because they had failed to go to the other place. In order to combat this feeling of "abandon hope all ye who enter here," the Headmaster of the Modern School had organised, among other activities, a School Eisteddfod. The children who felt themselves ignored now found themselves applauded. If they were bad at sums, they were good at singing ; if they couldn't spell, they could act ; if they couldn't satisfy the examiners, they could entertain an audience.

So much of the stage work devolved on the new Handwork Master that John Phillips the following year found himself appointed Secretary of the School Eisteddfod. He was a born organiser, and he enjoyed the work. When the National Eisteddfod came to Rhyd-yr-Onnen, he automatically became the unanimous choice of the whole committee for the post of Secretary. A special deputation waited on the Director of Education for the County, and John Phillips was given leave of absence for two years so that he could devote the whole of his time to organising the big festival.

The only thing John had against Rhyd-yr-Onnen was its distance from Liverpool. He was worried about Nancy.

The beauty parlour had weathered the first year fairly well, and Nancy forecast a marvellous increase in business for the second year. This did not materialise, but they were going to buy new machines shortly, and everybody knew, of course, that it takes at least three years to get a new business properly established.

The third year had come and gone. So had Nancy's partner, with a week's takings, leaving behind her a stack of unpaid bills. Nancy had sold the place, had lost three-quarters of her capital, and was now a receptionist at a hotel. She vituperated eloquently against her erstwhile partner, but had at last (she wrote) found a job just up her street. It was a lovely hotel, and the Manager was lovely, and the staff lovely, and she was having a lovely time.

John smiled wryly as he read her letter, and wondered when the next blow would fall. Her letters, however, remained jubilant, though John sometimes felt a strain of forced gaiety between the lines. Whenever he could, he went to Liverpool for a few days' holiday, and he and Nancy spent as much time together as her duties would allow. Lately, however, owing to the Eisteddfod job, they had not met as often, and there had crept into Nancy's letters a moodiness which he did not like. She had left the hotel which had been so full of loveliness, and was now receptionist at a much smaller hotel—and a much shabbier one, as John found. She and the Manager of the lovely hotel had quarrelled ; she did not say about what, but she couldn't possibly stay there any longer. She was getting less wages at this hotel, but she had more time off.

John went to see her, and was startled by the change in her appearance. She looked old and ill and haggard. With some difficulty, he persuaded her to take a week off and come back with him to Rhyd-yr-Onnen. Good country food, fresh air and peace and rest, would do her the world of good.

She came, was made very welcome by John's landlady, but the end of the week saw little improvement in her health. John could not understand her moods, the sudden bursts of joviality followed by such deep fits of dejection. It was with a sad heart that he saw her off on Friday. She was gay and happy as she kissed him good-bye, but had stubbornly refused to stay over the week-end, as promised. John couldn't help wondering how long the gaiety would last.

On Saturday, Sergeant Roberts came to see him. John had just finished his mid-day meal when he arrived.

"I waited until you'd had your dinner, Mr. Phillips," said the Sergeant. "I'm afraid I've got bad news for you— from Liverpool."

2. An Ugly Death

John Phillips pushed open the door of the shabby hotel where Nancy had lived and died. Inside the drab little vestibule, he hesitated a while, looking for a bell to ring. Then he heard footsteps coming down the stairs to his right. He turned and saw a tall young man wearing a belted raincoat and carrying a trilby hat. The young man smiled and came to him.

"Mr. John Phillips ?" he asked.

John nodded.

"My name is Lewis—Detective Sergeant Lewis, Liverpool C.I.D. I was afraid of missing you at the station, so waited for you here. Sergeant Roberts gave you the message about your sister ?"

"All he told me was that she had been found dead this morning," replied John.

"That's all we told him," said the detective. "We weren't sure then whether it was suicide or murder."

Suicide ? Murder ? The words didn't register at first : John heard them, but what had they to do with Nancy ? She had died suddenly in her sleep, said

Sergeant Roberts. They wanted him to go to Liverpool immediately. He could catch the three-fifteen and be at Lime Street Station by seven-thirty. Nancy was dead. And this man was saying something about suicide and murder.

The meaningless words gradually urged themselves on his consciousness. He repeated them to himself. They became significant and pregnant and ugly. The man was again talking to him.

"We've interrogated all the members of the staff, and the few people who were staying the night here. We're satisfied now that she died by her own hand. The Inspector is in the Manager's room upstairs, waiting for you. I'll show you the way."

Sergeant Lewis turned and went up the stairs. John followed him, his mind still in a daze. They turned left at the top of the stairs, and Lewis knocked at a door marked MANAGER. Somebody called "Come in," and Lewis opened the door.

"Mr. John Phillips," he announced. "Inspector Gordon."

John went in. The tall, burly man sitting in the armchair facing him rose to shake hands. John liked the feel of his hand, strong, warm, reliable.

"I'm glad you've arrived, Mr. Phillips," said the Inspector. "I realise what a terrible shock this must have been for you." He turned to the other occupant of the room, a short shiny man sitting in the armchair opposite. "Cohen," he said, with a rasp in his voice, "can you get a pot of tea for Mr. Phillips, and a sandwich or two ? He's had a long journey."

"Yes yes, yes yes," replied Mr. Cohen, jumping nervously to his feet. "Two minutes, two minutes only."

He bustled out of the room, and Sergeant Lewis closed the door after him.

"Sit down, Mr. Phillips," continued the Inspector, "and I'll tell you the whole story as we know it. It's a sad story, but I'm glad to say that murder doesn't enter into it. Suicide is bad enough, I know, but murder . . ."

126

He paused, waiting for John to say something. John searched vainly for words, licked his dry lips, and could find nothing to say.

The Inspector smiled sympathetically, and went on.

"At half-past seven this morning, the Manager of this hotel—the oily little specimen who has just gone out—rang up the Police Station to say that a girl working here had been found dead in her bedroom. She hadn't turned up for breakfast, and the chambermaid had reported that her bedroom door was locked. Cohen got the pass-key, and they unlocked the door and went in. Your sister was lying on her bed, fully dressed. She was dead."

At last, John found the words he had been seeking.

"May . . . may I see her, please ?"

"Yes," nodded the Inspector. "But let me finish my story first. Sergeant Lewis and I came here, and we saw that death was due to poisoning. We could also see that the poison used was strychnine. All the symptoms were there." He paused. "Death from strychnine is not a pleasant thing to see, Mr. Phillips, and you must prepare yourself for it. Being her brother, you will have to identify the body. I wish I could spare you the duty, but . . . would you like to get it over now, or would you rather rest a while ?"

John shook his head.

"I'll see her now, if I may."

"Right. Will you take him up, Lewis ? And I'll get Cohen to hurry up with the tea and sandwiches."

"I won't have anything to eat, thank you," said John. "But I'll be glad of a cup of tea."

"I'll see that it will be waiting for you," said the Inspector. "Don't let him stay there too long, Lewis. All we need is proof of identity."

John followed the Sergeant up another short flight of stairs, and along a narrow linoleumed passage till they came to a door at the end of the corridor. Lewis unlocked the door, and they went in. It was a very small bedroom, very sparsely furnished.

John looked at the bed, bracing himself for a shock,

and was relieved to find that what he saw was not as bad as the picture his imagination had painted. He had expected to see Nancy, her face covered with her usual heavy make-up, lying fully dressed on the bed. But somebody had washed her face, dressed her in a nightie, and put her to bed. Her eyes were closed, her hair combed. The lines of her face were still set in a mask of agony, and there were marks on her lower lip where her teeth had bitten deep into the flesh.

"It was an ugly and a painful death," said Lewis quietly, "but the doctor said that it was mercifully short, and that she couldn't have felt any pain after the first few seconds. She is your sister ?"

John nodded, without speaking. It was good to think that she had not suffered long. But how did the doctor know ? How could he tell ? Would she have bitten through her lip if she had not felt the pain ? What had made her do it ? She had joked and laughed and chatter-ed when she kissed him good-bye. Her depression had gone : she was alive, vibrant, the old Nancy that he had known and loved. Now she was dead. A suicide. An ugly and a painful death.

"That's all for now," said Lewis. "We'll go back to the Inspector. There will be an inquest on Monday, and you'll have to give evidence of identity. I've also arranged for the removal of the body, tonight at ten o'clock. We try to do these things as quietly as we can when death occurs in a hotel or lodging-house. I can give you the name of a firm of undertakers, if you like, who will see to all the necessary arrangements for the funeral. I've already contacted the firm, and the secretary will discuss the arrangements with you this evening. Will that suit you ?"

"Yes," said John. "Thank you."

Lewis opened the door, and John went out. He felt empty and void, and the words buzzing in his head drummed vainly against the emptiness inside him. He stopped in the passage, automatically drew out of his pocket a packet of Players, took out a cigarette, and put it in his mouth. He saw Lewis looking at him, and with a muttered word of apology, John offered him a cigarette· Lewis took it, smiled, and lit John's and his own.

The smile touched a chord that breached the void in John's heart. He realised suddenly that all this—the grimy hotel, the chipped linoleum, the oily manager, the Inspector in the room downstairs, Nancy lying dead in her bed—he realised that all this was real, really happening, and happening to him. As he followed the detective's broad back along the passage and down the stairs, he repeated to himself what he had been told and what he had seen.

The Inspector had heard them coming, and was pouring out the tea when they went in.

"All right ?" he asked.

"Yes," said Lewis. "It's his sister."

"Sit down, Mr. Phillips," said the Inspector, "and drink this while it's hot. Do you feel better now ?"

John nodded.

"Yes," he said. "I've got over it now."

"Good. The doctor said there's no need for an autopsy. There's no doubt at all about the cause of death. It was strychnine." He paused, and looked at John. "Tell me, Mr. Phillips, were you aware that your sister took drugs ?"

John was so startled by the question that his cup clattered in the saucer as he put it down.

"Drugs ?" he repeated. "No. I never thought that—"

He paused abruptly. Nancy's sullen fits of depression and her sudden fits of gaiety came to his mind. He remembered what he had read in books about drug addicts. What a blind fool he had been ! He could see it all now. But one never thinks of one's own sister as an addict. "No, I hadn't realised it. We haven't seen much of each other lately, not until this week. I could see that there was something wrong with her, very much wrong, but I never for a moment thought it was drugs."

"Cocaine," said the Inspector. "There's been a considerable increase in drug traffic since the war, especially in what we call the brown drugs, mostly opium and Indian hemp. It wasn't so easy to smuggle the white drugs because Interpol has been able to disrupt most of the traffic. But this year there has been a definite increase in the white drugs too, especially cocaine. And I'm afraid that before very long there will be an increasing traffic in other drugs that are superseding cocaine among young addicts in the States—cannabis, heroin and so on. Have you any idea, Mr. Phillips, where your sister could have got her supply of cocaine ?"

John shook his head. How could he know ?

"We've searched every nook and cranny in her room," continued the Inspector, "and failed to pick up a single clue. But she must have been getting supplies regularly from some source or other. We went through every stitch of clothing, searched every drawer, looked in every book, read all her letters. You were her only correspondent—at least, all the letters we found were from you. We've questioned all the staff, and they don't recollect her receiving any parcels by post. The drug must have been given her by hand. We've investigated the credentials of every guest who has stayed here during the week, and especially those who were here last night. We'll go on investigating, but so far we've learnt nothing new. We found some suspicious characters among the clientele of this place—ticket-of-leave men, a couple of prostitutes, one or two known pickpockets, and one fellow we suspect of being a fence, a receiver of stolen goods. But nothing at all to connect any of them with drug trafficking."

"May I ask a question ?" said John.

"By all means. What is it ?"

"Sergeant Lewis said that at first you suspected murder. Why ?"

"There were two reasons. A suicide usually seeks comfort in death. An old woman who kills herself in a gas-oven always has a cushion under her head. Your sister was lying on the bed fully dressed, with fresh make-up on her face, as if she had planned to go out somewhere. There was no preparation on her part for death. And secondly, she had chosen to take strychnine, the most virulent poison of them all. People who kill themselves with poison usually take a soporific, and death comes gently to them in their sleep. That is what made me think, at first, that the poison was not self-administered."

"May I ask what made you change your mind ?"

"We found the paper which contained the poison, and the only fingerprints on it were her own."

"But the murderer could have—"

"Worn gloves ? Of course. But there was a more positive reason than the lack of fingerprints. The chambermaid saw her go into her room at half-past nine last night and asked her, jokingly, if she was going to bed early for a change. Your sister laughed and replied that she was going out again soon. The chambermaid heard her lock the door, and thought she was going to change her dress or something. But this morning, the door was still locked, and the key still in the lock, on the inside."

"If my sister intended to go out, she didn't intend to commit suicide !" remonstrated John.

"Why lock the door then ? Not to change her dress. She was wearing the only decent dress she had. And the key was still in the lock this morning. The chambermaid tried to look inside through the keyhole, and couldn't. And when Cohen came with the pass-key, he had to push the key out of the hole to insert his in order to unlock the door. I examined the key very carefully under a microscope, Mr. Phillips, and there were no marks on its end as there would have been if somebody had turned the key by force, using a narrow-jawed pair of pliers, from the outside. The window was securely latched, and the dust on the sill outside was undisturbed. I am positive that nobody could have entered the bedroom to administer the poison. She died by her own hand. Did she intend to die ? That is something we do not know, Mr. Phillips. If she knew it was strychnine, she meant to die. But if she knew it was strychnine, did she also know that it would be a very painful death ?"

John clutched at a straw of hope.

"She may have thought it was another kind of drug, and have taken it by mistake."

The Inspector glanced at Lewis, and nodded.

"We've already gone into that," said Lewis. "It's a theory that we can neither prove nor disprove. Maybe your sister was getting to the end of her tether, and for some reason or other, probably because she had spent all her money, her supply of cocaine was running short. Desperate, she may have threatened to expose the person who supplied her. And in order to silence her, that person could have deliberately given her the strychnine and told her it was a new kind of drug. It's a possibility we have to bear in mind. But proving it in a court of law, without evidence to support it, would be impossible."

"We do know," added the Inspector, "that there's a new gang which has been particularly busy these last few months. We've caught two or three of the pushers, as we call them, the agents who distribute the stuff, mostly cocaine. But we're still searching for the head of the gang. Nor have we been able to trace the source of supply. So many ships come here from the Middle and the Far East that we can't possibly search them as thoroughly as we would wish. We make an occasional haul, but we know that a lot more passes through. When we catch the head of this new gang, he'll get the longest stretch the law can give him. We'll put him behind bars for the rest of his life."

"You think that would be sufficient punishment ?" asked John, quietly. "The man is a murderer. It may have been he who sent the strychnine to my sister. Doesn't he deserve to be hanged ?"

"If Lewis and I had our own way," said the Inspector, grimly, "we'd deal with him ourselves, and there would be no frills to his passing. It's a very good thing for both of us that we can't take the law into our own hands. The man may be as guilty as sin, but the Law demands that he must have a fair trial. When we do catch him—and he'll fall into the net sooner or later—he'll face a judge and jury, and he'll be put away."

"And yet get away with murder ?"

"If we could prove that he had sent the strychnine to your sister, telling her it was some other kind of drug, we could of course bring a charge of murder against him. But we'd have to do more than satisfy ourselves of his guilt. We'd have to satisfy a judge and jury."

"And he might get away with it ?"

The Inspector shrugged.

"Some do," he said. "There are murderers who have escaped the penalty of their crimes. You know how the Law feels about hanging—that it's better for nine guilty men to escape the rope rather than have one innocent man hanged."

Sergeant Lewis looked at his wrist-watch and rose to his feet.

"It's half-past eight," he said. "Would you like to see the undertakers now, Mr. Phillips ? I told the secretary you'd be there before nine."

John got up.

"I'd like to thank you, Inspector, for being so patient with me," he said. "When is the inquest, and where should I report ?"

"Ten o'clock, Monday morning. Lewis will come to fetch you. Are you staying at this hotel ?"

"God forbid," replied John. "I'll find somewhere else."

"There's a little hotel just off Dale Street which is clean and quiet," said Lewis. "I know the landlady, and I'm sure she can put you up for a couple of nights. It's quite near the undertakers, and we can call there on the way. Is that all right with you ?"

"Thank you very much," replied John. "Is that all, Inspector ?"

"That's all for the time being," replied Inspector Gordon. "This has been a sad affair for you, Mr. Phillips, and it would be absurd of me to tell you not to worry about it. You can't help worrying over a thing like this.

I know there's little consolation in believing that things could be worse, but I feel that I should tell you one thing. Your sister, had she lived, would have grown deeper and deeper under the influence of the drug. The end would have been a complete breakdown—physical, mental, moral. You have no idea, Mr. Phillips, how awful the ravages of cocaine can be. Your sister, believe me, was spared a worse fate. There are other girls who have suffered much more than she did."

3. The Bookmark

The inquest did not last long. Sergeant Lewis had forecast as much on the way there.

"Some coroners," he commented, "love the limelight, and make mountains out of mole-hills to get into the headlines. But this morning's coroner is a wise old bird. The Inspector has already had a talk with him, and they've agreed that there's no need to bring up the question of drugs. We want to find out, if we possibly can, where your sister had been before nine o'clock on Friday night. We think she had been out to meet the pusher who supplied her with cocaine, and that he gave her what he said was a new kind of dope."

"The strychnine ?"

"Yes. Mind you, the fellow who passed it on to her may also have thought it was dope. He may have been the instrument of her death, not the author. We'll have to catch him to find out. Anyway, we don't want the drug story to come up in court, in case he gets the jitters and leaves the district. We mustn't frighten him off. So the less said about it the better. You'll be the first witness called. The coroner will ask you to establish the identity of the body, and if you noticed anything wrong with your sister lately. Tell him about the fits of depression she suffered from, and that she worried a lot over the loss of her money in that beauty parlour business. That will be all he'll want from you. Then the doctor will describe the cause of death, and the Inspector will testify that the poison was self-administered. One of the jury may ask if she took the strychnine by mistake for something else, and the coroner will say that there was such a possibility, and for that reason he'd advise the jury to return an open verdict of death by poison, without committing themselves to any opinion on that score. If things go smoothly, we shouldn't be there more than an hour or so."

The Sergeant was right. Everything was over before eleven o'clock.

"Let's go across the road for a coffee," said Lewis when they came out. "The Inspector would like a word with you."

What Inspector Gordon had to say was short and to the point.

"I don't want you to leave Liverpool, Phillips," he said, "feeling that we're going to leave the case where it is. We've been on the track of this gang for some time, and sooner or later your sister will be avenged. I've got your address, and if anything breaks, I'll get in touch with you. I've also asked Cohen to send to me immediately any letters or parcels that may come for your sister. I hope you don't mind my doing this. I don't expect any, but one never knows. We do have a bit of luck occasionally." He turned to the Sergeant. "Lewis, if I give you the afternoon off, would you like to go to the funeral? I don't like the idea of Phillips being there on his own."

"Of course I will go," said Lewis.

"Good," said the Inspector. "I'd hate Phillips to go back to Wales feeling that we're a cold-blooded lot."

"I wouldn't do that," protested John, "you have both been very kind to me."

"Let's hope we'll meet again on a happier occasion." The Inspector rose and shook hands with John. "I suppose you'll be going to the hotel this afternoon to see about your sister's effects? If you have any trouble with Cohen—he's a slippery customer, is little Cohen—ring me up at the Police Station, and I'll put the fear of God in him. Good-bye, Phillips."

There had been no trouble with Cohen. What few effects Nancy had left were easily disposed of. Her account at the Bank had long been exhausted, every trinket of value had been sold, and John told the chambermaid to do what she liked with the clothes. He was glad to leave the place. Cohen gave him a clammy hand to shake when he finally left the hotel, and was obviously as pleased to see the last of John as John was to see the last of him.

John and Lewis, and the two men from the undertakers, were the only mourners who followed Nancy's body to the crematorium. John moved like a man in a dream, divorced from reality. The short service touched no chord in his heart. It was only when the coffin slid out of sight into the furnace awaiting it that he felt a sudden surge of wrath sweeping into his heart. He looked at Lewis, and saw in the Sergeant's face a reflection of his own anger. Lewis, like himself, was not thinking so much of the girl who had died as of the man who had killed her.

There was no mention of the inquest in the morning papers on Tuesday. In happier times, when the columns of a thirty-two page newspaper gaped for copy, the suicide of a silly girl in a shabby hotel might have rated a short paragraph. Today, she could not be spared a single line. Marshal Stalin had made a speech which could mean anything and might mean nothing ; England, after scoring over two hundred runs without loss before lunch, had been skittled out by Australia for 357 before close of play ; an American film actress who had married a French film actor on Saturday was already threatening to petition for a divorce, an intriguing situation full of hilarious possibilities. No, there had been no room for Nancy.

When John alighted at Rhyd-yr-Onnen station, he found Sergeant Roberts waiting for him.

"Inspector Gordon rang me up, Mr. Phillips. Suggested

we should have a little talk like. I'll walk home with you."

"It's like this, you see," explained the Sergeant. "Like every little town where everybody knows one another, Rhyd-yr-Onnen's chief recreation is gossip, and once a story starts on its rounds, there's no knowing how it will grow and when it will end. Inspector Gordon has told me what happened in Liverpool, but there's no need for anybody else to know about it, is there ? In fact, I've told Mrs. Jones Shop Chips—and it'll spread from there all over the town—that you were called to Liverpool because your sister had had a sudden seizure and died. Lots of people saw her here last week, and could see how ill she looked. Don't you go an' tell them any different, Mr. Phillips. Least said, soonest mended."

John had gladly followed his advice, and threw himself into the work of the Eisteddfod to try and forget what he had gone through. Miss Williams, his clerk, had had a very busy time during his absence. It was the first week in May, and all the literary entries had to reach the Eisteddfod Office before the seventh of the month. There were over thirty competitions in the literary section, and over six hundred entries had been received. All these had to be numbered, entered in the books, and posted to the adjudicators. In the major competitions, such as the Chair Ode and the Crown Poem, there had to be three copies of every entry, a copy each for the three adjudicators. For the remainder of that week, John and Miss Williams worked daily until the early hours of the morning.

John was so tired on Sunday morning that his landlady persuaded him to have breakfast in bed, a thing that John usually abhorred. A bath before lunch refreshed him, but he decided to give Sunday School a miss that afternoon, and to sit indoors and read. Never a great reader, he had no light reading available, and having finished the Sunday paper, he found himself wandering round the room looking for something else to read.

A paper-back novel with a highly coloured cover

depicting a manly looking male, in very short trunks, hugging to his hairy chest a lissome female even more scantily clad, brought a smile to his lips. Surely, his sedate landlady didn't read that kind of trash? Of course not, it was the book Nancy had been reading. He flicked through the pages, and a piece of paper fell out of it. He picked up the note, and read it :

Dear Nancy :
Don't be silly, darling. Threats don't mean a thing to me. I can't possibly let you have any more on tick. It's far too expensive. But I've got some cheaper stuff you can try. George will bring you a sample. Friday, usual place, 8.00 p.m.
Love,
David.

No date, no address, but he realised its significance immediately. This note proved that Nancy had not committed suicide. She had been murdered. She had received the letter on—when had she received it ? Which morning was it ? He remembered that she wasn't feeling too well that morning. He had taken a cup of tea to her bedroom. She wouldn't have anything to eat. The postman had just called, and John had nearly opened her letter with his own letters. A good thing that he always looked at the postmark before he opened a letter. This one had come from Shrewsbury, and he knew nobody in that town. He had taken another look at the address, and had seen that the letter was for Nancy, not for him. It was the only letter she had received all week. But which day was it ?

Friday, of course ! She had half promised to stay over the week-end, but when he came in for lunch, she had got all her things packed, and insisted on going back that afternoon.

He nodded to himself. Yes, he said, Inspector Gordon was right about the drugs. I can see it now. Her supply had got very low, and she was trying to eke it out to last the week. That's why she was so unbalanced. She was getting desperate, had threatened to expose the fellow who supplied her, and then this letter arrived, giving new hope of fresh supplies. She finished off what she had left, and was on top of the world when I came in for lunch. Too excited to read, she had used the note as a bookmark, and then forgot to take the book with her to read in the train. Thank God she did forget it ! Inspector Gordon would now be able to trace this David.

But would he ? He paused, doubtfully. There was no address, not even a signature. Even the name was typewritten. Well, what of that ? The C.I.D. could identify typewriting as easily as handwriting. No two typewriters are exactly the same. Letters wear unevenly ; some may slip out of true ; a bit of a letter gets cut off ; the lines become slightly crooked—there are dozens of little idiosyncracies which can prove on which machine a letter was typed. Take this note, for instance. Where's that magnifying glass I had ? Here it is. Look at the capital G in George. See ? There's a small bit missing at the bottom. Makes it look at first sight like a capital C, not a capital G.

And then, like a bolt from the blue, something hit him so suddenly that he ceased to think. Something had clicked in his mind with such force that it numbed thought. He found himself staring hard at that capital G. And slowly, gradually, another capital G with the same little bit missing took shape in the mirror of his memory. That other G was followed by an O and an E and a D. The whole word built itself up in his mind. It was GOEDWIG, the Welsh word for forest. Y GOEDWIG, that's what it was—The Forest. He had thought, when he had first glanced at it, that it was Y COEDWIG, and had laughed at it.

"Look here," he had said to Miss Williams, "here's a bloke competing for the Chair, and he can't even spell correctly !"

Then he had looked again at the word, and had seen that it was a capital G, not a capital C. A bit from the bottom was missing : the same bit that was missing from the capital G in George.

A coincidence ? Perhaps. He could easily find out. Every competitor in the Eisteddfod had to use a *nom-de-plume*. With his entry, he had to send a sealed envelope containing his real name and address. On the outside of this envelope he wrote the name of the section and number of the competition, the title, and his *nom-de-plume*. The poems and stories and essays and all the other entries in the literary section had been forwarded to the various adjudicators, but the sealed envelopes were kept in the safe at his office.

Were there any other peculiarities in this note ? Carefully, very carefully, he studied every letter through the magnifying glass. The capital D in "Dear" was not quite straight : it leaned slightly, very slightly, to the left. The small "t" also had a piece missing : the little stroke which should cut across its top had lost the bit on the left-hand side. He turned the note sideways, and looked along the lines of typewriting. The small "a" was not quite in alignment : it was a shade lower than the other letters.

He folded the note, put it in a clean envelope, and placed it in his pocket. He put on his hat, came back to the table for the magnifying glass he had nearly left behind, and went out.

Inside his office, he soon found the envelope he sought. There was, of course, no postmark on it. The envelope, together with three copies of the poem, had been enclosed in a larger envelope which he had not kept. On the outside of this sealed envelope was typewritten :

A : Barddoniaeth (Poetry)
1. Awdl Y Gadair (The Chair Ode)
Y GOEDWIG (The Forest)
Ffugenw'r Ymgeisydd (Nom-de-plume of competitor)
DAEDYLUS

He took out the magnifying glass, and studied the

typewriting with minute care. Capital G occurred three times, and each time the little bit at the bottom was missing. Capital D also occurred three times, and each time it was not quite vertical. Small "t" occurred once, and the left-hand crosspiece was absent. He turned the envelopes sideways, and looked along the lines of print. Small "a" occurred twice in the top line, and both times it was a shade lower than the other letters.

All this, said John to himself, cannot be a coincidence. It is proof positive that the note and the envelope were typewritten on the same machine.

Inside this envelope was the name and address of the man who had typed them. Nancy's murderer.

He pushed the pointed end of a pencil under the flap, and rolled it slowly downwards. As it rolled, the pencil gently pushed the flap open. He took out the half-sheet of paper inside the envelope, and read it :

> Daedylus—
> > David Beynon,
> > > The Wayside Inn,
> > > > Llanhelyg,
> > > > > Flintshire.

He compared the "David" on the note with the "David" on this paper. They were identical.

He had identified Nancy's murderer. All that he had to do now was to get in touch with the Liverpool C.I.D. David Beynon would be arrested, tried, and—

And what ?

There came back to him what the Inspector had said about murder and murderers. "We could bring a charge of murder against him," Inspector Gordon had said, "but we have to do more than satisfy ourselves that he is guilty. We have to satisfy a judge and jury. Murderers have got away with murder before now."

He had said something else too. What was it ?

"We'd willingly deal with him ourselves, Lewis and I. And if we could, there would be no frills to his passing.

It's a good thing for us that we can't take the law into our own hands."

All right then, said John to himself, I'll deal with him myself. I shall have no compunction about taking the Law into my own hands. Beynon deserves to die, and I shall see to it that he does. I must do it in such a way that no suspicion will hang over anyone else, and so carefully that I shall not be suspected myself. It will take time to plan it, but when the Eisteddfod is over, I shall have heaps of time to organise his execution. Yes, that's the word. Execution. It isn't murder. Not even revenge. It is simply getting rid of a creature that deserves to die. An execution.

But first of all he would have to make absolutely certain that Beynon was guilty. There was no doubt in his mind that the note and the envelope had been typed on the same machine. But it did not follow, however, that the same person had typed them. The same typewriter, yes ; but the same typist ? Some other person might have had access to the machine. How could he find out ?

There was only one way. He would have to go to The Wayside Inn to make inquiries. Llanhelyg wasn't very far by road, only a couple of hours' run on his motor-bike. But, having arrived there, how could he make inquiries about the typewriter ? He must think of a pretext—Ah ! The very thing ! Nothing could be simpler.

Soon after he had been appointed Eisteddfod Secretary, a salesman from a typewriter firm had come to see him. The man was going round all the offices in the district to do minor repairs to typewriters. Or so he said. He had examined John's machine, and had made a small adjustment to the tension of the spring. John had successfully resisted the man's attempt to sell him a new machine, and had offered to pay for the adjustment. The man had laughingly refused payment, and had confessed with a smile that the repairing was only a bait : his real job was to sell new typewriters. When there was anything seriously wrong with a machine, he would give the owner an estimate of the cost of repairs, but would strongly advise him to trade in the old typewriter in part exchange for a new model.

Well, said John to himself, I know enough about typewriters to do any minor adjustments. Except for the alignment, there doesn't seem to be anything seriously wrong with the machine which typed the note and the envelope. I couldn't do anything about the broken letters : I'd have to tell him to send the machine to the firm who made it to get the letters replaced.

When can I go there ? Now that we've sent out all the entries, I can take a half-day off this week. Let's see. I've got committees on Monday, Tuesday, and Wednesday, but I'm free on Thursday. Good. I'll go there after lunch on Thursday.

But I mustn't rush things. I must keep cool. As cool as a cucumber, my father used to say, but not so green. Remember, he'd warn me, that if you want to be a good carpenter, you must have three things. The first is patience ; the second is patience ; and the third is patience. First, the patience to make sure that you get the right wood for the job : you can't make a right job with the wrong wood. Then the patience to make sure that your measurements are accurate and exact : the difference between a joint and a gap is the thirty-secondth of an inch. And lastly, the patience to make sure that you cut out the right bits : you're done for if you don't. A writer can rub out his mistakes ; a doctor can bury his ; but a carpenter has to pay for them. Take time, trouble, and care.

I shall, vowed John. When I'm absolutely sure of Beynon's guilt, I shall kill him very very carefully.

4. The Plan

Sarah Powell, the elderly housekeeper at The Wayside Inn, liked the looks of this young man. He was different from the crowd which came there nowadays. This one treated her with the respect due to her age, this one did, not shouting at her like the others, and making fun of her to her back. A very nice young man he was, and had even insisted on her having a drink with him, which she never did with strangers really, because you can't be sure who anybody is these days, can you ? But it had been such a hot and tiring day, and those plasterers had left such a mess in the kitchen that it would take her and the maid at least two more days to clear it up proper like. All this painting and decorating was too much for her at her age, indeed it was, and if the new owner expected her in addition to stay up half the night cleaning up after his silly parties after spending the whole evening cutting sandwiches, then he'd have to find another housekeeper before long, she wasn't going to be put upon, not if she knew it, so there.

John had listened with patience and well simulated interest for over half an hour. He had gleaned quite a lot of information about David Beynon during this time. When he had inquired for him, and had been told by Sarah that Beynon was away from home, John was at first afraid that he had come on a fruitless journey. But listening to Sarah had caused him to revise this opinion. He would never have learnt from Beynon as much as he was now learning from Sarah.

He had learnt, for example, that David Beynon had bought the place last January, and had completely renovated it, and now the commercials who used to stay there never came near the place, and the old customers from Llanhelyg had changed over to The Plough, and Sarah didn't hold with all this drinking and dancing

144

every Wednesday and Saturday night. And—most significant of all—he had also learnt that David Beynon spent much of his time away from the hotel. Sarah didn't know what his business was, nor where he went, but a friend of hers living in Shrewsbury had seen him there on Thursdays.

"Every Thursday?" asked John.

Sarah wasn't sure about that, but he was there last Thursday whatever, and the Thursday before that, too.

The Thursday before, thought John. That was the day when Nancy's letter had been posted. And the postmark was Shrewsbury. A small clue, but it fitted. A little link in the chain.

"About these girls who come here on Wednesdays and Saturdays," John had asked her during their chat, "do they come from the places around here, or from a distance? A girl from Liverpool was telling a friend of mine last week that she had been to a party in a little inn in North Wales. I wonder if she meant this place? Her name was Nancy something. I don't suppose you remember her, Miss Powell?"

The old lady shook her head. She didn't know where the people came from, but it wasn't from around here, she knew that. She did remember a Nancy something who had been there once or twice. But not lately, though. She remembered her because she was Welsh. Quite a decent girl, too, though she drank and smoked more than was good for her. Yes, she could speak Welsh.

"She told me she'd been living for some time in Anglesey," added Sarah. "She had a grandmother there who kept a little shop. Left her some money, she said."

That settles it, said John. And now, what about the typewriter?

"I wish somebody left *me* some money," he smiled. "My job is quite interesting, but not very well paid."

Sarah pricked up her ears. Had John told her outright what his job was, most probably she'd have taken no notice. But his oblique reference to it aroused her feminine curiosity. She was too polite, however, to put a direct question.

"Yes," she nodded, "I always do say that you commercials make a hard living. Not half so easy as some people make out."

"I'm not exactly a commercial traveller, Miss Powell. I'm a mechanic who repairs typewriters. That's why I called. I was hoping that there was a typewriter here which I could have a look at, and—well, you know, get it adjusted and cleaned up. There's always some little thing wrong with them, but they're too heavy and bulky to be sent away for minor repairs. People are usually very pleased to see me for this reason, and I'm very sorry to hear that Mr. Beynon isn't here. I suppose he's got a typewriter ?"

"Yes, it's in his office. He doesn't use it much, though. He isn't at home long enough to use it a lot, if you ask me. But I haven't heard him complain of anything wrong with it."

"Probably there isn't," said John. "Is it a new one ?"

"Oh no, it was here before he came. He bought it with some of the other fittings."

"Could I have a look at it ?" asked John. "If it's alright, it will save me the trouble of coming here again. And if there's anything wrong with it, I could drop Mr. Beynon a line to tell him how much it would cost to put it right."

Sarah shook her head.

"Sorry," she said. "It's too heavy by far for me to carry it here."

"No, no !" expostulated John. "I wouldn't dream of asking you to bring it here. But you could perhaps spare five minutes to take me to see it ? All I want to do is to type a few words on it. It wouldn't take me a couple of minutes to see if there's anything wrong with it." He smiled at his most winsome. "If there is, it might mean a little job for me, you know, and I'd be glad of the chance to earn a few shillings."

Sarah hesitated. This young man, after all, might be a

146

burglar for all she knew, even if he didn't look the part. She was just going to refuse when the door of the lounge opened and Constable Jones came in. His entrance solved her problem.

"Sit ye down, Jones," she said, "and I'll draw you a pint o' beer. This young man has come to see the typewriter in the office. We won't be a minute."

The typewriter was an old Remington, very much used, but still usable. John slipped an old letter into the machine, and typed the three rows of letters, small and capital, on its back. He could study them later.

"It's a very old model," he said, "and I'm afraid there's nothing I can do except try to persuade Mr. Beynon to buy a newer model. Does anybody use the typewriter besides him ?"

Sarah shook her head.

"No, he's the only one."

"He hasn't got a secretary ?"

"Good gracious, no ! What would he be doing with a secretary in a small place like this ?"

"And he never lends the typewriter to others ? Nobody comes here to type—"

"Nobody. He's the only one that uses it, and he doesn't use it much."

"In that case," said John, "there's no point in my coming to see him. This old machine will last him for years if he doesn't use it much. I'm very glad you let me see it : it's saved me coming here again. Thank you very much, Miss Powell."

He shook hands with her, thanked her profusely once again, and left.

Back at Rhyd-yr-Onnen, he tried to tabulate the results of his visit to The Wayside Inn. What had he established ?

1. Nancy's letter and the sealed envelope were both typed on the machine kept at The Wayside Inn.

2. The only person who used this machine was David Beynon.

3. Nancy's letter was posted at Shrewsbury on April

147

30th. David Beynon was in Shrewsbury on that date.

4. Nancy knew Beynon, and before her money was exhausted had attended at least one of the parties at The Wayside Inn.

5. Beynon spent four days every week on secret business away from home.

6. Inspector Gordon had said that drug trafficking had been rampant during the past few months. Beynon had come to The Wayside Inn in January. So remote a place was ideally situated for the headquarters of a gang of distributors.

Any one of these clues, by itself, might not be sufficient to convict Beynon. But evidence accumulates by geometric, not arithmetical, progression. You don't add clues, said John to himself, you multiply them. A clever counsel, however, might be able to convince a jury that a case built on circumstantial evidence was not absolutely foolproof ; he could appeal so strongly to their fear of convicting an innocent man that he might be able to frighten them into acquitting him. But so far as I am concerned, said John, I am convinced that Beynon is Nancy's murderer. What I do not know is how many other girls he has driven to their death.

I shall kill him, he resolved. Not now, and not for some time. I shall have to plan it well beforehand, to the smallest detail. I'll find out where he spends the time he is away from home. I shall shadow him for weeks if necessary. Then I shall pick the best time and the best place for the execution. I shall wait until the days shorten before I kill him, and I shall be very careful that I am not caught. And now—patience ! I shall do nothing more until the Eisteddfod is over and done with.

This last resolution he did not keep. An opportunity arose which he could not resist.

Early in July, the three adjudicators of the Chair Ode informed him that they had agreed on their verdict. The winner of the Chair was DAEDYLUS. They did not know who he was. Nor did anybody else, except John.

He alone knew that the Chair Bard was the man he had sworn to kill.

The sealed envelope he had opened had been re-sealed by him. When the adjudicators' decision reached him, he called the Eisteddfod Chairman and the Eisteddfod Treasurer to his room. The Eisteddfod Executive Committee had already agreed that the best way of keeping secret the identity of the winner was to confine the knowledge to these three officials. John opened the sealed envelope in their presence, and told them who DAEDYLUS was. Beynon himself would not be informed of his success until the week previous to the Chairing. The Treasurer or the Chairman would go to The Wayside Inn to tell him. This was done to ensure the Bard's presence at the Chairing Ceremony.

The idea of killing Beynon during this ceremony came to John when the Committee was discussing the ceremonial costumes. A purple-red robe had to be provided for the Bard. He would be invested in this robe before he was escorted to the stage.

Purple-red. The colour of blood. A robe of this colour would conceal any bloodstains.

It was so fantastic an idea that John thought no more about it. But that night, waking unexpectedly in the small hours, he found himself thinking again about the purple-red robe. His subconscious brain must have been wrestling with the problem in his sleep. Before he got up that morning, his plan was complete.

Beynon would be shot. The weapon used would be the high velocity automatic which John had been able to bring with him from Germany. It was a lovely gun, about eight inches long, and it could kill at fifty yards with a .22 bullet. If he could get near enough to Beynon to make sure of shooting him right through the heart, there would be very little blood. If any did seep through his jacket, the purple-red robe would hide the stain.

But a gun makes a noise and shows a flash. How could the noise be drowned and the flash hidden ?

He had a silencer for the gun. But was that enough ?

The safest way of drowning a noise is to make a louder noise. Would the noise of ten thousand people shouting HEDDWCH at the top of their voices drown the noise of the shot effectively enough if he fitted a silencer to the gun ? It would prevent the shot being heard by anyone standing a few yards away. But what of those in the immediate vicinity ? Even if the sound was only a small pop, they would still hear it.

And they would certainly see the flash. He couldn't hide the flash from them. Of course, it wouldn't be a very big flash. Not as big as those the press photographers would make, but it was—

The press photographers ! There would be a score or more of them kneeling in front of the stage. If he knelt among them, he would be surrounded by flashes. A battery of flashes. One more flash wouldn't be noticed among so many.

John smiled. He knew now that there was no need for him to wait until after the Eisteddfod to kill Beynon. He would never get a better opportunity than this. He already had the gun and the silencer and the bullets, and nobody knew he had them. All he needed in addition was an old camera, or a wooden box which could be made to look like a camera. He could easily make one. The gun would be fitted inside the box. He could fix it in such a way that he could aim the gun when he looked into the view-finder. The muzzle of the gun would point at the hole where the lens was supposed to be. The trigger would be controlled by a small lever at the side of the box. The same lever would also light the flashlight bulb fitted on top of the box. A small blob of solder placed at the base of the bulb would short-circuit the current and cause the bulb to explode when lighted. Any photographers kneeling beside him, if he happened to see the flash and hear the pop of the gun, would believe that it was the bulb which caused them. He would grin sympathetically at John, and then turn hurriedly to the stage to take more pictures of the collapsing Bard. In the commotion, John would sling his fake camera over his shoulder, rush to the stage to see if the fellow was really dead, and help to carry off the body. And then, when the Eisteddfod was over, he'd go far far away from Rhyd-yr-Onnen and get rid of gun and camera. It was a marvellous plan. It couldn't fail.

On this last morning of the Eisteddfod, smoking his first cigarette of the day, John Phillips repeated the words to himself. It was a marvellous plan. And it hadn't failed.

5. Picture Gallery

Back at their own hotel, the Chief turned grumpily to Hopkyn.

"I'm not a bit happy about that Cadwaladr fellow," he grumbled. "He was a damn sight too cocky. Blast the man ! I thought we had the case sewn up, and now we're no nearer a solution ! Are you quite sure, Hopkyn, that Emlyn Cadwaladr couldn't have done it ? Those alibis of his were too vague for my liking. An elderly minister called Jones, and a young couple called Tom and Dilys ! Much too vague, Hopkyn !"

"That's why I believed his story, Chief. A guilty man makes sure of his alibis. He can produce them on demand. Cadwaladr didn't even know his. No, we can safely acquit Cadwaladr. He had a motive, but it wasn't he who murdered Beynon."

"Motive, yes. And opportunity too. The report from Preston said that a high velocity automatic can kill up to seventy-five yards, and he was much nearer to the stage than that !"

Hopkyn shook his head.

"I'm not at all satisfied, Chief, that anybody sitting in the audience could have fired the shot without being seen and heard by his immediate neighbours. No silencer can drown the noise of a shot so completely that the man in the next seat wouldn't hear the pop, even if there were ten thousand people shouting HEDDWCH at the time. And there's the flash, too. A silencer doesn't hide the flash of the shot. The people sitting near would certainly see it. Tell me, Chief, is there anything in the papers this morning about the shooting ? The news hasn't leaked out ?"

"Not a word in the couple I've looked at. Yesterday, while you were away, Hopkyn, I got Sergeant Roberts to buy me copies of all the papers, and I went through every one of them in case any rumour of the shooting had leaked out. And then, Hopkyn, I . . . er . . ." the Chief sounded rather apologetic as he went on, ". . . I thought I'd do a little detective work on my own. Reconstruction of the crime, as it were. One of the papers had four photographs, taken within a second or two of one another, and they'd arranged them in a strip across the front page. I cut the strip out. Wait a minute, I'll fetch the cutting. I'll bring the others too. Won't be a minute."

He bustled off with his usual haste. Hopkyn smiled abstractedly, still turning over in his mind the puzzle of the sound and the flash. He wasn't at all interested in the Chief's pictures, but he had better humour the Old Man.

How to conceal the pop and the flash—that was the problem. How the devil could they be concealed ? The pop and the flash.

The Chief had returned, and was busy arranging a pack of photographs, each one mounted on stiff card-board, on the table. Hopkyn regarded him without interest, immersed in his own thoughts.

"This is what gave me the idea, Hopkyn, these four photographs. See ? One, *The Smile of Victory* ; two, *The Pang of Pain* ; three, *The Bard's Collapse* ; four, *Final Exit.*" The Chief snorted in disgust. "Morbid, Hopkyn, morbid ! Leaves a bad taste in the mouth. But, all the same, they made me think. So I got together all the papers, and cut out all the pictures. Then I tried to arrange them in sequence, see ? Some of them were taken at the same instant, of course, and I chose the best of

them. But there's a lot of others with a split-second difference in the timing, and I thought that if I could arrange
them in the order of their taking, I could then build up a
slow-motion picture of the murder. See what I mean ?
Jolly good idea, I thought. What d'ye think of it ?"

"Excellent," murmured Hopkyn, and went to the
table to have a look at the Old Man's work.

The Chief had worked hard at his idea, and the
pictures—one following the other at split-second intervals
did give a slow-motion picture of the murder.

First time I've ever seen it done in a murder case,
mused Hopkyn. Usually, we have to wait until the
murder is committed before we can start taking photographs. But this time there were a score or more of
photographers actually present when the murder took
place, and the Bard died to a bombardment of flashes.

Of flashes. A bombardment of flashes. One more flash
wouldn't be noticed in a bombardment. If the murderer
were crouching among the photographers . . . but could
he have been kneeling among them ? The bullet had
entered the body just below the heart. Then it had passed
through the left ventricle into the backbone. So the shot
had come from below. It could have been fired by someone kneeling among the photographers.

But the stage was full of people. Surely, some of them
would have noticed a man aiming a gun at the Bard ?

Unless the gun was camouflaged. Fitted into a box
which looked like a camera. A .22 high velocity automatic
is only eight inches long. Fit a flashlight on top of the
box, to go off simultaneously. The flash of the bulb
would hide the flash of the gun.

Ah ! But there would still be a little noise, a little pop
even with a silencer attached to the gun. The audience
wouldn't hear it in all that shouting. The people on the
stage wouldn't hear it. But the photographer kneeling
alongside the murderer would certainly hear it, and the
strangeness of the noise would draw his attention.

The strangeness of the noise ? But it wouldn't be a
strange noise to a photographer ! How many times had

he heard Sergeant Rawlings, the fingerprints expert at the Yard, swear like a trooper when his flashlight bulb popped ? And it's easy to short-circuit a bulb to make it pop. A small blob of solder would do it. Or a bit of wire. Even a piece of silver paper. Stick it between the legs of the bulb. And then, when it is switched on, there's a flash, a pop, and the bulb's gone.

"Chief," said Hopkyn, "your photographs have solved at least one puzzle. I know now how the murder was done, and I've got you to thank for it. Listen."

6. Final Curtain

The Chief listened with rapt attention to Hopkyn's exposition. When it was finished, he jumped to his feet and clapped Hopkyn enthusiastically on the shoulder.

"Splendid, Hopkyn ! A most ingenious scheme, and it was darn clever of you to think of it !"

Hopkyn grinned.

"It was the murderer who thought of it first, Chief. And it was you who made me think of it. Those photographs were a brainwave."

The Chief fingered his moustache and coughed self-consciously.

"Very good of you to say so, my lad. I'm very glad indeed that I've been able to help. At my age, the old brain doesn't function very quickly. Hrmph ! I really don't know what made me think of cutting out those photographs. In fact, I felt rather a fool playing about with a pair of scissors and a pot of gum. Oh, well !" A note of complacency came into his voice as he squared his shoulders. "Now we know where we're going !"

"Not so fast," grinned Hopkyn. "We've discovered how Beynon was shot, but we have still to find out why he was shot and who did it."

Some of the swagger went out of the Chief's shoulders, and he sat down again.

"Damn ! I was still thinking of that fellow Cadwaladr. And he is a press man, Hopkyn ! You're absolutely sure he couldn't have done it ?"

"Absolutely," replied Hopkyn, with a finality that the Chief could not question. "But now that we have discovered the method, it may not take us long to discover the murderer. Manners maketh man, said Bacon, and the method often betrays the criminal. One can very often tell who broke into a house by his method of entering it."

"That's all very well," grumbled the Chief, "with habitual criminals. They get into a rut, as we all do. But there's nothing habitual about murdering the Chair Bard of the National Eisteddfod of Wales."

Hopkyn laughed aloud.

"Don't you ever tell me again, Chief, that the old brain doesn't function. You've hit the nail on the head. What makes murder a more difficult puzzle to solve than most crimes is the fact that as a rule it's only committed once. Anyone who makes a habit of it gets caught, like the Smith fellow who drowned his wives in a bath. But even in a single case of murder, such as this one, the method employed may betray the killer. Beynon's murderer had planned an ingenious method of committing it, a method that I've never seen used before. But all the same, like many another criminal, he has left behind one clue so obvious that he didn't see it. He was so absorbed in the mechanics of the crime, so careful of the little details that were to ensure its success, that he forgot the most obvious clue of all, the very clue that would lead us to him once we had discovered his method."

The Chief stared at him incredulously.

"Do you mean to tell me, Hopkyn, that you actually know who the murderer is ?"

"Not yet," replied Hopkyn, "but I hope that I shall know very soon. I am still in the dark, however, about the motive. I know that it isn't legally necessary to prove motive in a case of murder, but a jury always wants to know why it was done, even if the judge warns them that it isn't essential. It would strengthen our case considerably, Chief, if we could discover the motive for the murder."

"We've already done that," expostulated the Chief. "The stolen poem."

"The stolen poem provided a motive for Emlyn Cadwaladr, but not for anybody else. We can forget the poem. The only clue we have is the left-luggage ticket— and the bank books. What time is it, Chief?"

"Just gone eleven."

"I was hoping that the Liverpool C.I.D. would have rung up before now. Ah!"

There had been a knock at the door, and Hopkyn looked at it expectantly. The door opened, and Mr. Price Jenkins, the Eisteddfod Treasurer, came in. Hopkyn's face fell : he had expected Sergeant Roberts with a telephoned message from Liverpool.

The Treasurer had his own private worry. No relation of the dead Bard had turned up to collect the prize money. Nor was there anybody to take charge of the funeral arrangements. The body was still in the hospital mortuary, and the Matron wanted to know who was responsible for its disposal. As Treasurer of the Eisteddfod, he had taken it upon himself to order a coffin from the local undertaker, and had provisionally fixed the funeral for Monday afternoon. But it didn't seem right for a stranger like himself to decide the final arrangements. Could the police help in any way ?

"As far as we have been able to find out," explained the Chief, "the only relative is a half-brother who will have nothing to do with the dead Bard. And the only suggestion that I can make, Mr. Jenkins, is that you carry on until someone turns up. Somebody will have to see that the fellow is put underground, and if nobody else is interested, the Eisteddfod Committee had better take over the job."

"In that case," said Mr. Jenkins, "I shall make the final arrangements, taking your sanction as official permission to proceed. I can discuss the financial details later on with the deceased's legal representative, and I shall hand over the ceremonial details to my colleague,

Mr. William Rowlands, the Chairman of the Committee." A wintry smile flitted over his face. "He will doubtlessly enjoy the publicity."

Hopkyn grinned. He liked the Treasurer's icy humour.

"Tell me," he asked, "did you have any difficulty in getting the Chairman to keep quiet about the shooting ? He struck me as the last man on earth to be trusted with a secret."

"Mr. Rowlands," said the Treasurer, "has one ambition in life, and one only : that people should look up to him. He is quite capable of keeping a secret if it is clearly explained to him that he will become the laughing-stock of the community if he dares to divulge it. You may have noticed, Inspector, that the identities of both the Crown and the Chair Bards were very well kept this year."

"They were indeed," agreed Hopkyn. "Did the Chairman know who they were ?"

"The Executive Committee very wisely resolved that the only safe way of keeping the names a secret was to confine their identities to the main officials only—the Chairman, the Secretary, and myself. We knew early in July who had won the Crown and the Chair, and we kept the knowledge strictly to ourselves. I had taken the precaution of warning the Chairman that he would be publicly sacked from the Chair if he disclosed the names."

"You say that the three officials were the only ones who knew the names. Is that quite right, Mr. Jenkins ? What about the printers of the book ?"

"They were not informed until the very last moment, when the list of winners had to go to press. Well, gentlemen, I shall now bid you good morning. The Male Voice Competition is on this afternoon, and the Secretary and I will be extremely busy for the next hour or so. Good morning to you."

The Chief saw him out, closed the door after him, and grunted.

"He's as human as a sausage machine, Hopkyn."

"I like him," laughed Hopkyn. "And both of us should

feel particularly grateful to him this morning. He's just told us who the murderer is."

"What !"

"You heard what he said. You should know now who shot Beynon."

The Chief's brow furrowed in thought for a moment. Then he gasped.

"Good heavens ! I'd never have thought of it ! William Rowlands of all people !"

"No, no, no," chuckled Hopkyn. "I could perhaps imagine William hacking somebody's head off with a chopper, but he hasn't the brain to plan so ingenious a murder as this one. The man who murdered Beynon was Phillips, the Secretary."

"Phillips ?"

"Of course it was. You see, Chief, this murder was planned in advance. Very carefully planned. Therefore the murderer must have known in advance that Beynon had won the Chair. The Treasurer, after I had fed him with some leading questions about William's powers of secrecy, assured us that the only persons who knew in advance that Beynon had won the Chair were the Chairman, the Treasurer, and the Secretary. The Chairman and the Treasurer were sitting at a table on the right hand side of the stage when Beynon was shot. They sat on his right hand, but he was shot through the heart, so they couldn't have done it. The only one of the three who could is Phillips. That's what I meant just now when I said that the murderer had left a very obvious clue. The method adopted for killing Beynon proved that the murderer must have known in advance that Beynon had won the Chair."

"Of course ! Simple, Hopkyn !"

"It always is," smiled Hopkyn, "when explained. Being a Handwork Master at the school, Phillips had both the tools and the ability to rig a camera. And as Secretary, he was on and about the stage so much that people didn't notice him. Like Chesterton's postman, he was taken for granted."

"But what was his motive, Hopkyn ? Why did he kill Beynon ?"

"I can only guess at his motive, Chief. I can't prove it without making further inquiries. You remember what I told you last night about the left-luggage ticket ?"

"You said it was a useful method for a thief to pass on loot to a confederate without having to meet him in person."

"The last time I came across it was when a ship steward was caught smuggling watches from the Continent. He put them in a suit-case, left the bag at Victoria, and posted the ticket to a confederate living in Birmingham. But I don't think Beynon dealt in watches. His profits were too large. Now then, Chief, you know as well as I do that there's one commodity which you can smuggle in very small quantities and sell for very big profits."

"Dope. Cocaine, for example."

"Cocaine, heroin, Indian hemp, opium, morphine, *etcetera.* Cocaine happens to be the most popular. If I'm not very much mistaken, the bag left at Lime Street station contains cocaine. That's why the drawer in Beynon's office was full of small envelopes, and why he spent four days a week away from home. The problem, however, will be to trace the connection between Phillips and the drug traffic, but perhaps . . ."

A knock at the door cut him short.

The door opened, and Sergeant Roberts came in. He saluted the Chief, and came straight to the point.

"Telephone message from Liverpool C.I.D. to Inspector Hopkyn, sir. I thought at first that Inspector Gordon was pulling my leg. Tell Inspector Hopkyn, he said, that he was right, and that the bag was full of snow." Roberts laughed. "I didn't catch on. Snow in August ? Then I remembered, of course, that snow is slang for cocaine." He paused a moment, looked rather doubtfully at the Chief, and added, "Inspector Gordon was asking after Phillips, too. I mean the Eisteddfod Secretary."

Hopkyn sat up.

"Oh. Did they know each other ?"

Roberts was hesitant. The Chief lost patience.

"Come on, man ! Speak up. Why did Inspector Gordon inquire after Phillips ? Out with it !"

"It happened three months ago, sir. I didn't put it in my official report : it was something confidential between Phillips and me. You see, sir, Phillips had a sister living in Liverpool. She was a drug addict, and committed suicide. Inspector Gordon—"

Hopkyn had jumped to his feet.

"I'll get on the phone with Gordon immediately, Chief. Quick, Roberts, ring him up for me. Hurry, in case he leaves the station. I'll follow you." Roberts hurried out. "Chief, this looks like the final curtain. But there's one thing more that I'd like to lay my hands on. The camera. Phillips hasn't had much time to get rid of it, and we should make an effort to find it. The Treasurer said that he and Phillips would be busy at the Eisteddfod for the next hour or so. Could you go to Phillips' lodgings, and persuade the landlady to let you search his room ? There's time to get a search warrant if you think it necessary."

"Right !" said the Chief. "Send Roberts there after me. If the camera's anywhere in the house, we'll find it !"

They did. Phillips had felt so safe that he hadn't even dismantled it. It was in the bottom drawer of his desk, the first piece of furniture they searched.

When they returned to the Police Station, Hopkyn had got all the evidence he needed. He told the Chief what he had learnt from Inspector Gordon.

"It's a cast-iron case, Hopkyn. Congratulations !"

Hopkyn did not reply. The Chief looked at him.

"What's wrong, Hopkyn ? You don't seem very pleased. Good God, man, this is the end of the case !"

Hopkyn sighed.

"Yes, the part I hate. All my sympathies are with Phillips. Beynon is better dead, and the world is a cleaner place without him. Now, thanks to me, Phillips will hang for it." He smiled wryly. "Gilbert was right, Chief. A policeman's lot is not a happy one."

"You're right, lad," said the Chief. "It's a hateful job to arrest a decent young man like Phillips for killing one like Beynon. But we've no choice in the matter. He may be reprieved, after all. Oh, well ! Come along, Hopkyn. Let's get it over."